Just How Things Are

Cary Duane

RED PLANET PUBLISHERS

To those who understand just how things are.

CHAPTER ONE

The Fitting

T he muslin felt warm from the sun.

Madison stood still on a low pedestal, arms slightly out, chin level, while the tailor circled her like a gull orbiting the tide. Pins glinted between his lips. A measuring tape slithered over Madison's ribs, hips, collarbone. She did not flinch when the fabric was tightened or when a pin pressed too close. That, she had learned, was unseemly.

Vivienne, her mother, sat nearby, cross-legged and flawless, a linen notebook in her lap. She was nodding at nothing—just the general shape of things—because it would never be enough for her daughter to be merely acceptable. And especially not today.

"Raise your arm," the tailor murmured coldly.

Madison did as she was told. A silent, obedient offering. The sleeve caught on her wrist bone and was adjusted.

She could hear the distant waves through the windows, mingling with the sharp snips of thread. Boats would be out already. White sails waving like linens hung out to dry in the wind. She would rather have been out there with her father—bare feet on the deck, book in her lap, while the surf whispered against the hull. He'd let her read in peace, then draw her out with questions about the story—always genuinely curious about what she thought.

"Soften the waist," Vivienne said. "She's only a child."

Madison didn't speak. She rarely did at fittings. Her opinions didn't matter—not here, not when the dress was never really for her. It was for the others: her mother, her aunts who fussed, even her grandfather, who noticed everything and complimented nothing. They would remark about how she was growing, comment on her posture, her shoes, the fit of the sleeves. Worth was measured in details, and missteps were discussed in whispers.

The tailor squinted. "Turn."

Madison turned. She angled herself just the right amount—not too fast and not too mechanically. The silk itched beneath her arms where it hadn't been lined, but she didn't move to scratch. She had learned long ago that stillness made the dress look better, and looking better made everything easier.

The tailor made one last adjustment at the hem, murmuring something under his breath as if the fabric might listen. Then he stepped back, hands on hips, surveying the silhouette like a sculptor weighing the balance of a nearly finished piece.

Madison caught a glimpse of herself in the mirror. A girl in pale pink silk, her green eyes steady, auburn hair pinned perfectly with care. She looked like she'd been created— a porcelain doll on display.

The silence lingered, just long enough to feel staged. The tailor paused, waiting for Vivienne's next instruction. Then—

A knock at the studio's side door broke the pause, light and casual. The tailor startled slightly. Vivienne didn't flinch.

The door creaked open.

"Is this where they're holding my daughter hostage?" a voice asked—smooth, amused, and just a little out of breath.

Madison turned before she was told. "Daddy!"

Alaric La Croix stepped inside with the smell of sun and sea still clinging to him. His sleeves were rolled, his jacket slung over one shoulder, and his dark hair had that care-less, wind-touched look that drove photographers mad. He stopped just a few paces in, the light catching the fine lines at the corners of his eyes.

"Look at you," he said softly. "Maddie—you're stun-ning."

The smile bloomed before she could stop it. Wide, bright, full of awe and trust.

Vivienne cleared her throat, a subtle warning. "She still needs to be pinned—"

"Let her breathe," Alaric said, waving a hand. He walked slowly around the pedestal, eyeing the dress like it might come to life and waltz away with his daughter. "It's a bit much, isn't it? Aunt Mattie will have opinions."

"She always does," Madison said, softly.

Alaric laughed. "That's my girl. Still sharp beneath all this silk."

Vivienne clicked her pen once—crisp, deliberate—but said nothing.

The tailor backed away, sensing the shift in tone. This wasn't about hem lengths anymore.

Alaric stepped closer and rested a hand gently on Madison's shoulder—fully hers in that moment. The weight of his hand felt real, unlike everything else in the room.

"You nervous about today?" he asked, more gently now, and sincere.

Madison gave a small shrug. "No. Just… tired of holding my arms out."

Alaric crouched so their eyes met at the same height. One knee touched the floor, like he needed to be closer to her level to cut through the weight of everything else in the room. "So, what will it be today? Let me guess—we make our entrance, grandfather inspects his progeny, praises the lineage, criticizes the shoes."

Madison nodded. "And I say thank you even if I hate the dessert."

"Perfect." He winked. "You'll do just fine."

He stood again, gently brushing a stray thread from his cuff. A lull settled—until Vivienne closed her notebook with a snap and spoke, too evenly.

"She needs to make a proper impression, Alaric. Today isn't about desserts or clever remarks."

He didn't meet her gaze but smiled reassuringly at Madison. "She'll be fine."

"You always say that. And then you leave me to smooth over the details. Your daughter makes a joke, and you praise her for being witty. I correct it and become the villain."

Alaric exhaled slowly, finally turning toward his wife. "What do you want me to say, Vivienne? That she's not enough? That we need to cinch the waist tighter, so she looks more like a lady?"

Vivienne's jaw tightened. "I just want her to be ready."

Madison blinked once, her smile fading. The porcelain surface remained, but the warmth behind it cooled.

Alaric's voice softened again. "She's ten. Let her be ready in her own way."

Neither parent spoke for a moment. The room was suddenly too quiet, too still—until the tailor gently cleared his throat.

Madison resumed her position without being asked.

CHAPTER TWO

The Gathering

Madison stared silently at the bows on her shoes, wondering if they were the kind a duchess would choose.

The gravel crunched beneath the tires as the car pulled through the gates. Madison's hands folded in her lap, the silk of her dress brushing against her knees each time they turned. She could see the house now—tall and white, its windows catching the sun like polished bone. The hedges were trimmed to unnatural precision. The flag on the lawn barely stirred.

Vivienne adjusted her pearl earring and looked straight ahead. "Let your grandfather greet you first. Hands at your sides. And if he comments on your posture—"

"I'll correct it," Madison said quietly.

Alaric glanced at her in the rearview mirror, catching her eye. He didn't smile this time, but there was a flicker of something—understanding, maybe. Or an apology.

They parked beneath the portico where the stones stayed cool, even in summer. The car barely slowed before a footman stepped forward with the precision of a stage cue. Vivienne stepped out first, her hand gliding along the frame of the door as if the moment were being watched. She paused to smooth her skirt, eyes scanning the entryway, then turned and offered Madison a hand—steady, practiced, almost ceremonial.

Inside, the air smelled of beeswax, lilies, and salt. Every surface gleamed. A chandelier shimmered above the entry hall, its crystals catching the light like icicles. Portraits of ancestors lined the walls—stern men, corseted women, eyes that never quite met your gaze. A butler appeared and nodded, then turned and led them toward the terrace where guests had already begun to gather—men in pressed linen, women in soft pastels, laughter too refined to rise above a murmur.

Madison kept close to her mother, silently counting her steps to match Vivienne's pace. She recognized a few faces from past holidays and portraits in the hall. A woman with silver curls gave her a thin smile. A girl about her age glanced over, then quickly looked down. Near the hedge, an older boy leaned against the stone edging, listening to a man who did most of the talking. Two women nearby compared scarves with grim intensity, as if something depended on the outcome.

Alastair La Croix sat beneath a striped umbrella at the edge of the terrace, a tall glass of water beading at his side. He wore a pale summer suit, hair white and immaculately combed, his expression carved more from habit than interest. The crease in his trousers held sharp despite the heat, and a signet ring caught the light as he shifted. Even seated, he looked as if he were presiding—over the estate, or the gathering, or both. His gaze held the same cold authority as the portraits in the entry hall: disapproving, inevitable. When he saw them approach, he rose—not quickly, but deliberately.

Vivienne gave Madison the faintest nudge.

She stepped forward, hands at her sides, then dipped into a small, formal curtsy—the kind Miss Hilliard had drilled into her after breakfast for weeks. "Hello, Grandfather. It's good to see you."

He looked her over—no words, just a sweep of the eyes from her shoes to her pinned hair. A pause. Then: "You've grown."

Madison inclined her head slightly. "Yes, sir."

"Turn."

She turned. Slowly, just as she had in the studio from before. The terrace had gone quiet behind her. She didn't look at anyone else. Looking would've made it worse.

Alastair finally gave a small nod and gestured toward an empty chair beside him. "Sit."

Madison obeyed. Her pulse was steady now. The worst of it had passed.

Vivienne took the seat to the other side, her hands folded neatly. Alaric remained standing behind them, his eyes on the water beyond the terrace, like he wished he were out there instead.

"It's a modest dress," Alastair said, after a while. "Restrained. Not too loud."

"Thank you, Grandfather."

Vivienne nodded once, careful not to overstep. "We try to consider the tone of each gathering when choosing the wardrobe."

"Consideration is easy," he said. "Consistency is where most fail."

Any hint of praise had dissolved by the time it reached her. Vivienne folded her hands tighter in her lap.

Madison looked down at her own hands, resisting the urge to pull at a loose thread along the hem.

And then, like a sudden gust off the harbor, came the sound of heels clicking against stone.

"Alastair, you old basilisk!" A woman called out. "If you're done measuring the girl like a prize ham, I'd like to say hello."

Madison looked up.

Aunt Mattie swept onto the terrace in a sun-yellow blouse with dramatic sleeves. Her patterned trousers clashed cheerfully with everything else on the terrace. Her hair was tucked under a wide-brimmed hat, and her lipstick was entirely too bold for the occasion. She carried a martini in one hand and a lacquered fan in the other.

Just behind her trailed her husband, Harrison—tall, courtly, and largely ornamental. He wore a pale blue cravat and nodded politely to each person they passed like a man shaking hands at his own retirement party.

Alaric smiled—truly smiled—for the first time since they'd arrived.

"Aunt Mattie," Alaric said dryly. "You're late."

"Fashionably," she replied, kissing him on the cheek.

Her gaze bypassed Vivienne and settled on Madison. "My little Maddie, you've gotten taller. I disapprove." She leaned over to give her a peck of her own.

Madison grinned before she could stop herself.

Vivienne's lips pressed into a line too thin to cast a shadow. "Mind her dress," Vivienne said, voice slightly pitched at the end.

"Nonsense," Mattie replied, settling herself beside Alaric and raising her glass. "If a dress can't survive a little life, it's not worth wearing."

Madison's smile lingered, smaller now, but still real. She watched the way Mattie's presence disrupted the air—how even Grandfather's grip on his glass shifted ever so slightly. Mattie didn't enter rooms so much as tilt them off balance—laughing too loudly, moving too brightly, never asking permission. Not everything had to be still, she realized. Not all power had to be restrained.

Mattie wasn't really Madison's aunt, at least not directly. Her given name was Matilda Beatrix La Croix—Alastair's youngest sister and an unmovable part of the family mythos. She had married Harrison Renshaw, a well-groomed but mostly passive figure who followed her through life with grace. They had no children—whether by choice or fate, no one had ever dared to ask.

Alaric had called her Aunt Mattie since he could speak, and everyone else followed suit. She hadn't earned the right to needle Alastair or breeze past expectations. She was simply born with it. Draped around her like a shawl.

And no one challenged her. No one ever had.

"I see you've all arranged yourselves like a portrait," Mattie said, flicking open her fan. "Do we smile on three or wait for the oil to dry?"

Alaric chuckled. Even Madison let out the hint of a giggle—quickly stifled.

Alastair gave no response.

"Where's Vivica's boy?" Mattie asked after a pause, tilting her head toward the crowd and then back to Alastair. "Surely you've trotted him out, haven't you? I assume the plan is to make him the heir apparent—unless someone else in this family manages a miracle."

Vivienne gave a tight smile. "He's speaking with Edward."

"Pity," Mattie said. "The boy's got wits as dull as a butter knife, but he photographs well enough. I guess that's what matters, isn't it?"

She turned to Madison. "Don't worry, darling. You have sharper eyes than all the men here combined. That's what counts."

She could feel the weight of Mattie's eyes on her, steady and exact, like they could see through all the composure and posture.

"She's ten," Vivienne protested.

"All the better," Mattie replied without blinking. "No one sees you coming when you're wearing pretty shoes with bows."

Madison looked down at her shoes again. She didn't know what to say. But the words stayed with her.

Alaric offered Mattie a new drink without asking. She accepted it with a familiar nod.

The day moved on, as did the conversation, drifting toward politics and restoration funds and the summer art series at the wharf. Madison kept quiet, watching, and listening. Every gesture. Every silence. The way her grandfather never looked at her twice once Mattie arrived. The way Aunt Mattie's attention always circled back to her.

She smiled once more, but no one saw it.

CHAPTER THREE

The Duchess

The formal shoes were off by the time Madison reached the stairwell.

She carried them by their straps like they might kick her if she let them swing. Stocking feet on polished wood made no sound as she slipped past the formal parlor, the marble foyer, the grandfather clock that always struck just a second too slow.

No one stopped her. No one called her name.

Lucille was already in the kitchen. She always was.

The scent of warm bread and freshly churned butter mixed with something earthier—maybe bay leaves—filled the air. The kitchen windows were open, and a gauzy curtain flapped through the sill like it was trying to escape. Madison hovered in the doorway, uncertain for just a second.

Lucille turned from the sink, hands still damp. "Well, if it isn't the duchess herself."

She'd started calling Madison *duchess* years ago—after a storybook she used to read aloud in the evenings, when the house was quiet and the air felt gentler.

The duchess in the story had been bold and clever. A little too proud, but always one step ahead. Madison loved her. She asked for the book again and again, even after she'd memorized every word. The nickname had stuck, long after the stories fell away into memory.

Madison beamed. "You knew I was back."

"I always know when there's silk on my stairs." Lucille dried her hands on her apron, then opened her arms. Madison stepped into them without a word.

Lucille smelled like flour and thyme and a faint trace of burnt sugar—the kind that lingered ever since she scorched a pecan pie and insisted it was intentional. She hugged Madison just tight enough. No pins. No posture. Just warmth.

"Did he like the dress?" Lucille asked, eyes curious.

Madison shrugged. "He said it wasn't loud."

Lucille snorted. "High praise from that one."

Madison pulled back, perched herself on the tall stool by the butcher's block, and gave a sideways grin. "Aunt Mattie came."

"Lord help us! And the roof's still on the house?"

Madison laughed—hair loosening, face soft, less porcelain in the golden spill of late afternoon light. With Lucille, there was no performance to keep up, no perfect etiquette required. Here in the kitchen, she was allowed to breathe.

While Madison watched, Lucille sliced something and set it on a plate beside her. Bread and cheese. A welcome snack.

"Did your mother say anything on the way home?"

Madison shook her head, tearing a piece of bread with her fingers before answering. "No, she was quiet."

Lucille raised her eyebrows but didn't speak, her expression shifting for a breath—knowing and protective. Then it softened into something warm and familiar as she took a piece of cheese for herself.

They ate in silence for a while. The refrigerator hummed. Somewhere beyond the kitchen, a sprinkler started up—distant, but rhythmic. The light through the window pooled across the floor, soft and undisturbed, as if even the sun knew better than to raise its voice here.

"You'll outgrow this house one day," Lucille said gently, breaking the calm. Her eyes were soft but distant, like she was seeing something years ahead and already missing it.

Madison looked up. "What do you mean?"

Lucille gave her a tender squeeze. "Just that one day they'll see you like I do."

Madison wanted to ask more, but she didn't. Some truths could wait.

So she dangled her feet and ate her cheese and bread. She wasn't a duchess right now.

Just a little girl.

Chapter Four

The Game

S t. Catherine's smelled of varnish and chalk dust—like memories trapped in time.

Madison knew the sound of its hallways well: the rhythmic tapping of shoes on lacquered floors, the squeak of a turning heel, the murmur of giggles trailing behind whispers. Laughter clung to the lockers, a trace of joy embedded in the wood grain, waiting to be stirred up again.

Her classroom was all tall windows and narrow desks, with grooves worn smooth by generations of restless hands. Pale blue walls gave the illusion of calm. Above the blackboard, a delicate script spelled out virtues: Patience, Diligence, Grace—each letter looped with old-fashioned care, as if manners were stitched into the wall itself.

Miss Allerton stood at the front, reading from a book about early explorers. Her voice was steady but distant, like she was more in love with the past than the girls in front of her. Madison followed along, but only loosely. Her eyes wandered.

Lydia Montgomery sat one row over, braiding her hair into a crown. Her fingers moved with practiced ease, like she'd done it a hundred times before—and she had. Lydia was one of those girls who seemed born knowing how to draw attention: always a little louder, a little brighter, a little more daring than the rest. Her braids were never just braids—they were declarations.

She'd once gotten in trouble for wearing a striped bow in her hair that wasn't part of the approved uniform. But the teachers never stayed mad at her long. Lydia had a way of smiling through reprimands, making even discipline feel like admiration in disguise.

On the other side, Abigail Dunn kept her notes in perfect lines, each crease deliberate. She never used the margins and always sharpened her pencils to the same length. Abigail had a mind like a filing cabinet—precise, compartmentalized, and quietly formidable. She wasn't loud. But when she spoke, it was usually to correct a fact or clarify a rule. The teachers trusted her. And the girls knew she had answers, even if they didn't always like them.

Madison sat between them—one girl full of fire, the other full of order. She didn't mind their intricacies. In some ways, she was like both of them. A spark that could draw every eye and a calm certainty that could hold them.

When the bell rang, the girls poured out into the spring light. They moved in practiced clusters, like birds in a shifting flock. Lydia led their trio toward the wide lawn, talking nonstop, her voice rising above the others and occasionally drawing glances from onlookers. Abigail followed, methodical as always, planning each step. Madison walked in the middle, quiet, listening, watching.

They settled under the old tree, its roots raised like a warning. The grass was dry and thin, but they called it theirs.

Every group had a spot—unspoken but fiercely defended. The older girls claimed the garden benches, where they traded secrets in low, knowing tones. The athletic ones gathered near the gym wall, stretching and laughing like they owned the breeze. A few loners carved out space by the fence, backs against the stone as if guarding the edge of the world. But this tree, with its warped roots and patchy shade, belonged to them.

"Truth or dare," Lydia announced, collapsing into a cross-legged sprawl. "But no dares. I'm not licking anything today."

"Truths only," Abigail agreed, giving a sharp glance to ensure the three of them arranged themselves in a careful triangle—equal distance, just so. "And no skipping. If you pause too long, you have to tell two."

Madison sat down carefully and adjusted her skirt properly, folding it neatly beneath her knees before placing her hands in her lap.

The questions started light: favorite colors, favorite teachers, favorite foods. Giggles sparked easily and faded quickly. Lydia exaggerated everything. Abigail corrected everyone. Madison listened.

When Madison's turn came, she didn't flinch.

"Truth," she said.

Abigail tilted her head. "What's something weird that you do?"

Madison looked up and pondered. The sun filtered through the branches above, warm and dappled. Caught on one of the limbs was a stray ribbon—faded, wind-frayed, forgotten. It dangled like a ghost from some older game, a silk remnant of secrets once told and barely remembered.

"My mother makes me wear gloves when I eat peaches," she said. "She says it's improper to get the juice on my hands."

A small silence.

Then: laughter. Not cruel. But delighted.

Abigail squinted, genuinely curious. "Does she make you wear them for other things?"

"Sometimes," Madison said. "When we have seafood. Or when guests come over."

"That's kind of fancy," Lydia said, holding her hands out in front of her, fingers arched delicately in midair. She turned them slowly, pretending to admire invisible gloves.

"It's not fancy," Madison murmured. "It's just how things are."

She didn't say it rudely. Or with a twinge of arrogance. She said it the way her grandfather might have. Calm, distant, final.

For a moment, no one said anything. They just looked at her. Not with envy. Not in awe. But like something important had just happened.

The game eventually moved on. The circle loosened. The giggles flickered in and out. But something in the air had changed that day. And Madison noticed.

Both of the other girls were reaching while she stood still. That was the difference.

She hadn't meant to impress them. But she did.

Just by being herself.

CHAPTER FIVE

The Schedule

Madison's day began before the sun had fully cleared the fog from the water. A soft knock at her bedroom door, always at six-thirty sharp.

Lucille entered without speaking, pulling back the curtains in a single practiced sweep. The room filled with pale light. Madison was already sitting up, hands folded across her lap, eyes still heavy but open. She had been awake for a few minutes, listening for the knock.

"Morning, Duchess," Lucille said cheerfully. "Up and at it."

By seven, she was dressed. She made her way downstairs to the breakfast room, where a quiet table was already set. No crumbs. No syrup. Nothing sticky. She ate with a cloth napkin tucked at her collar and her posture perfectly straight.

Her mother would be there, usually sipping something sparkling and flipping through a glossy magazine—floristry, interiors, whatever matched the season and didn't require much thought. Occasionally, her father appeared, offering a quick hug and a whispered joke just for her before vanishing into the day.

Then the schedule resumed.

At seven-thirty: French. No one she knew actually spoke it. Not even her cousins in Quebec. But the La Croix's had spoken French for generations, so Madison did too.

At eight-fifteen: posture and poise drills in the sunroom—measured steps, timed pauses, and the discipline of stillness. She practiced standing without fidgeting, eyes forward, fingers curved like they held importance.

At nine: she left for school.

Compared to the morning, school felt like a kind of freedom—even if it followed a schedule of its own. There were bells instead of chimes, teachers instead of tutors, and the occasional chance to laugh without correction. It wasn't rest. But it was motion.

She returned home at three, uniform pressed, shoes scuffed only slightly. Lucille met her at the door with a fresh dress and a brush for her hair.

Then the schedule resumed.

At three-thirty: piano. Miss Hilliard sat beside her with a metronome and a pencil, tapping out rhythm with quiet precision. The keys were always cold at first, like everything else in the house that waited to be touched.

At four-fifteen: correspondence—writing thank-you notes and signing birthday cards for relatives she'd never met. Occasionally, there were condolence letters, dictated by her mother. Each one a ritual in politeness, presided by a fountain pen.

Just before five, the light in the parlor had gone soft. Miss Hilliard was seated beside Madison, reviewing a page of penmanship with a frown just beginning to settle. Then the knock came—not sharp, not loud, but breaking rhythm. The door opened before either of them could speak.

Her father stood there coyly.

"Rescue mission," he said, holding out a wrapped mint from the parlor tray.

Miss Hilliard stiffened. "Mr. La Croix, we're in the middle of—"

"She'll return with all limbs intact," he said, with a smile too polite to challenge.

Miss Hilliard hesitated. Then looked back to Madison, as if weighing whether further resistance was worth it.

Madison rose with a suddenness that betrayed her usual poise. A strand of hair tumbled from behind her ear, falling freely.

They walked the long path behind the garden. She still wore her late-day dress, pale and stiff. He kept pace with her steps, not the other way around.

"Learn anything useful today?" he asked.

"I learned not to speak if there's citrus on the table."

"Brilliant," he said. "That'll come in handy next time you dine with the Queen."

Madison smiled. Real. Bare.

As they continued, he told her about the harbor—how the fog rolled in so thick that morning it had swallowed the dock. He described it like a story, not a weather report. He had that way about him. He never asked if she understood; he just assumed she did.

When they returned to the house, Miss Hilliard was waiting with her next lesson. Alaric gave her a wink and vanished down the corridor.

Then the schedule resumed like nothing had happened.

At five-thirty: art appreciation. Miss Hilliard unrolled reproductions of oil portraits and landscapes, pointing to brushwork and composition with the edge of a ruler. Madison copied brushstrokes in silence, surrounded by faces that never blinked and scenes no one remembered.

Dinner was served at seven—citrus-glazed fish with white asparagus. Madison wore gloves.

She had moved through the day like a figure in a snow globe—admired, contained, untouched.

That night, Madison lay in bed beneath pressed linens, the window cracked just enough to hear the garden fountain.

She didn't think about the schedule.

She thought about the flowers on her mother's magazine. About Abigail's face when Lydia licked a snail. About the thick, chilly fog drifting in from the ocean.

And how her father's voice made it sound warm.

CHAPTER SIX

The Sea

Weekends were different.

The structure remained, in a way—there were still calendars to be consulted, social events to attend, and outings carefully slotted between obligations. Some weekends brought luncheons with the daughters of business partners, or gallery events her mother insisted upon. Other times it was a brunch with the cousins from Providence, a get-together that always felt more like diplomacy than family.

Every once in a great while, there were larger family gatherings. Grand affairs, the kind of events that required extra staff and more polish. The ones they hosted were the worst. Her mother would rehearse pleasantries and straighten table settings that were already straight. She wore the stress like overly strong perfume—visible, cloy-ing, and impossible to ignore.

But that wasn't every weekend.

Sometimes, if the tides were right and the sky promised clear weather, the boat would be waiting.

Riding in the yacht wasn't always a grand affair. Not every trip involved caterers or crystal glasses or the hov-ering presence of staff. Some days it was just the three of them—Alaric, Vivienne, and Madison—sailing past the jagged rocks toward open water.

On those days, her mother would soften. Madison would catch glimpses — a glance that lingered too long, a laugh that escaped reposed lips. Madison's eyes would catch it all, curious but quiet. She didn't always under-stand what passed between them, only that it felt rare. Her mother might giggle — startled and light — and then quiet herself, smoothing it away like a wrinkle in her dress. Almost as if joy itself was something that needed to be tidied up.

Madison remembered those moments. But what she remembered most were the other trips.

Just her and her father.

Her mother would watch from the terrace, waving with a pale hand and a glass of something in the other. Madison never asked why she chose to stay behind. She just waved back from the boat.

Before they left the dock, Madison would always take off her shoes. Alaric called it her sailor's superstition, but she liked the feel of the wood under her toes—cool, worn smooth by sun and salt.

They had their own quiet rhythm before setting out. He'd loosen the ropes while she checked the cooler, both moving in practiced silence—each knowing what came next without needing to say it.

Setting off always felt like slipping into another world. The dock would fall away, the shore would soften, and ahead—just sky and water, blue folding into blue.

When they cleared the inlet, they would pass a red-leaning buoy bobbing off to port. Alaric called it "Sir Reginald," the stoic guard of the bay. He wore his tilt like a badge of honor and, according to Alaric, had never let a scoundrel through. They saluted him with great seriousness each time, their hands raised in mock ceremony before smiles blossomed.

At sea, he told stories—tales from his own childhood, sailing with his father, or strange ports he claimed to have visited. Some were surely exaggerated, filled with pirates and hidden treasure, but Madison never asked which parts were real. That wasn't the point. It was the way he told them, hands moving with the rhythm of the sea, voice low and sure.

Once, they saw a school of dolphins rise and vanish in the distance, leaping like skipped stones along the horizon. He pointed them out with a boyish grin, swearing they brought luck.

Another time, he let her steer for nearly an hour. He guided her hands at first, gently, then stepped back and let her take the helm. She held the wheel steady, proud, while he watched, smiling that quiet, soft smile she never forgot.

They played games, too—spotting shapes in clouds, or making up names and stories for distant boats they passed. Some had grand adventures mapped onto their rusted hulls, others carried secret cargo or whispered messages between islands. Alaric would always wave, as if he knew every captain.

Often, they would simply sit. Madison would pull a book from her canvas bag and read it aloud to her father, her voice soft against the breeze. Other times, she read quietly to herself while her father hummed beside her, the two of them wrapped in separate stories but drifting through the same world.

It wasn't silence like at the house—tense, composed, and correct.

It was silence that simply let you in, that welcomed you.

Out here, there were no rules. No posture lessons, no piano scales. Just the sound of the sea and the steady presence of the man who, in those moments, seemed to hold the entire world in his hands.

And she loved it.

But the return always came too soon.

When they neared the dock, the sun had soaked her into a quiet drowsiness—cheeks flushed with salt, hair tousled by the wind. She'd linger in the final stretch, hoping to slow it somehow, but the shoreline always came. The light would shift, the breeze would cool, and the day—like all things—would quietly end. The boat would be tied, and the spell would break.

Back to shoes. Back to the schedule.

CHAPTER SEVEN

The Shifting Floor

Something was different today.

Madison didn't know what.

The routine hadn't changed. Not really. The same quiet footsteps down the same polished hall. The same knock at exactly six-thirty. But the inside of her skin felt a little too tight.

She was almost twelve now. Not quite a child, not yet anything else. And no one had said a word.

The women around her—Vivienne, Miss Hilliard, even Lucille—had simply adjusted the margins. Her dresses were longer. Her shoes stiffer. Her freedoms narrowed to fit.

No one explained the heat that flushed her cheeks without cause. No one named the heaviness in her chest that came and went like the weather.

She dropped her fork twice at breakfast. The second time, it clattered onto the plate. Vivienne's fingers tightened on her glass, the faintest ripple in her composure. Madison pretended not to notice, but the room felt colder.

During French lessons, she stumbled over words she should've known—simple ones. Miss Hilliard's mouth pursed, but she didn't correct her. The silence stretched instead, heavy with implication. Madison straightened, heart pounding, more afraid of being dismissed than punished.

Even at school, things landed differently.

At recess, she laughed at something Lydia said—a joke about boys—and the sound escaped her throat in a pitch she didn't expect. Too loud. Too bright. A few heads turned. Lydia grinned, unbothered, but Madison felt eyes on her from the benches, the prickle of attention she didn't want. She ducked away, cheeks burning

In history, she raised her hand to answer a question but stumbled over her own sentence. Abigail, seated beside her, quietly whispered the correction under her breath. Madison wanted to glare, to swat her away, but instead she shrank back, the words drying in her mouth.

In the bathroom between classes, Madison stared into her reflection above the sink. Her face wasn't any different, but something about her eyes looked... off. Like they were a curtain and she didn't know what was behind it. She blinked once, then twice, hoping to catch a glimpse of what was hiding. When a pair of girls came in, giggling, Madison dropped her gaze and slipped out before they could take notice.

By the time she got home, something inside her was frayed. Lucille met her at the door with a fresh dress and a brush for her hair. Madison stood still and let her work, but she didn't meet her eyes. Lucille hummed softly as she brushed, filling the awkward silence.

At piano, Madison played her scales and arpeggios. Her fingers stumbled. She missed a key.

"The keys are too cold," she said. "That's why."

Miss Hilliard didn't look up from the score. "Then warm them with grace."

Afterward, she sat alone in the reading room, a book open but unread on her lap. The sun had dipped below the garden wall, casting long shadows across the floor. One of the roses outside the window had wilted early—its petals drooping like her thoughts.

Madison skipped dinner that evening. Vivienne didn't approve. Skipping a meal was gauche, a sign of disorder—but she didn't press the issue. At least not tonight. She simply looked once at the empty chair, then returned to her wine.

Later, Lucille brought her a snack. A small plate of sliced apples and cinnamon. It should have been a kindness. It should have helped.

"I didn't ask for this," Madison said.

Lucille blinked. "It's your favorite."

"I said I didn't want it."

Lucille set the plate down gently. "But you haven't eaten much today, Duchess."

Madison stared at the apples; her face hot. Her fists curled in her lap. She didn't want to eat. She wanted to throw them across the room.

"I'm not hungry!"

She pushed them to the edge of the table a little too forcefully and they fell to the floor like windfall fruit—ripe, sudden, and unwanted.

Lucille knelt to pick them up. Her voice was gentle. "You don't have to shout. Not at me."

But Madison had already turned away. She sat at the edge of her bed, jaw tight, staring out the window where the last light bled from the sky. She could barely make out the dark shape of the garden below, and the faint shimmer of the ocean in the distance.

She didn't understand. Not the heat. Not the anger. Not the guilt that followed.

She thought about the duchess from Lucille's storybook—the one who found keys, crossed thresholds, and faced the world with chin held high. Madison didn't feel like that. She didn't feel brave. She didn't feel like Lucille's duchess. She felt like a balloon someone had let go of—drifting, untethered, disappearing from view.

Later that night, long after the house had gone still, she lay awake with her thoughts. Wondering if she were broken like a toy someone had played with too hard, then left behind. A question floated into the dark, barely louder than a whisper.

"Why am I like this?"

No one answered.

CHAPTER EIGHT

The Empty Horizon

Alaric noticed the change.

He had been up early that morning, long before the house stirred. The sea air clung to the windows, fogging the glass in soft halos as he made his way down to the kitchen. He brewed the coffee himself—he liked the quiet ritual of it, a small rebellion against being waited on. The clink of the spoon, the hiss of steam, the weight of the mug in his hand—all of it reminded him of simpler mornings from a different life.

He stood at the window, watching the pale light spread over the lawn and the hedges Vivienne insisted be sculpted into shapes that seemed to resist their own growth. There was a peace to it, but also a loneliness. He had been feeling that more lately. Like his home had become a showpiece—tidy, polished, and missing the life that once filled it.

He found himself glancing down the hallway expecting to hear her footsteps—the little girl's slap-slap of bare heels on tile, the breathless laugh chasing after a forgotten question. He could almost hear her voice, bright and breathless. She used to wake the house with her energy, filling it with her light.

But these days, her presence clung like an old photograph—still there, but faded at the edges. A reminder more than a reality. Hints of her, but never quite her. As if the real girl had drifted out to sea, just beyond reach, vanishing into a fog where no one else could see her.

At first, he blamed it on school. Then on her mother. Then, silently, on himself.

He had hoped today would be different.

But she wouldn't look him in the eye that morning. Her hair hung in her face, slightly damp from the shower, though neatly brushed and tucked behind one ear. She stirred her food like it had wronged her. When he kissed the top of her head, she didn't flinch—but she didn't lean in, either. That was new.

He watched her for a moment longer, weighing his words, then set down his coffee with quiet care. "What do you say we get out of here? Just you and me. Clear our heads. A few hours on the water—might do us both some good."

He paused, trying to smile. Watching in anticipation for a flicker of interest, a softening.

She didn't answer. Her spoon clinked against the side of the ceramic bowl, rhythmic and aimless, like she was stalling for time. She kept her eyes down, focused on the swirl of fruit and yogurt, pretending not to hear.

Alaric tried again, gentler this time. "Come on, Maddie. Just us. Like before."

Finally, she looked up—but not at him. Past him. Through him.

"I don't want to," she said flatly.

Alaric blinked, trying to keep his voice steady. "Listen, I know something's been off. I thought maybe—"

"I said no!"

There was heat in it now. Her voice trembled, not with fear but with a fury she didn't yet understand. He opened his mouth, hesitated, then closed it again, the words falling away before they could form. She pushed back her chair with a scrape far too loud for the quiet room and stood with a brittle sort of grace.

"Excuse me," she said, barely above a whisper, and turned. Her bare feet made no sound as she disappeared down the hallway, leaving behind only the echo of something broken and unsaid.

He took a step toward her, a hand half-lifted, unsure if it was to stop her or comfort her—but she was already gone. He stood there a moment longer, stunned by the finality of it. Not the refusal, but the distance behind it. There was something happening inside her, and he couldn't reach it. Something had shifted, and she had walked away without a second thought.

He didn't know what to do with the silence now. The house felt completely foreign. Heavy with quiet and disappointment. He needed movement, the illusion of purpose. And the sea—well, the sea had never asked anything of him.

So, he left.

Madison had run to her room the moment she turned the corner, the anger in her chest folding into something softer, something messier. She closed the door with a quiet click, then collapsed onto her bed. The sobs came hard, sharp, as if they'd been waiting all morning to escape. She buried her face in the pillow, not to muffle the sound, but because she didn't want to hear it herself.

Eventually, the tears slowed. She wiped her face, sat up, and smoothed the covers with the backs of her hands. Composed herself. That was what she was supposed to do—compose herself.

Then she crossed to the window, arms crossed tight across her chest. She tried reading, flipping half-heartedly through the pages of a book she used to love, but the words slipped past her. She paced once or twice, circled the room without purpose, then sat down again. The quiet of the house pressed in from all sides.

And then, she saw it.

The white curve of the boat, cutting slowly across the blue, growing smaller and smaller with each second. She watched it vanish into the horizon; teeth clenched hard.

She didn't know why she was angry. Only that she was. That he was gone, and she hadn't stopped him.

But she should have.

Chapter Nine

The Waiting

Saturday night settled over the house like a breath held too long.

Madison had brushed her hair twice through, refastened the silk ribbon at her collar, and repositioned the lamp by the window so it cast a warmer glow. She told herself she wasn't waiting. But she was.

She kept glancing toward the hallway, listening for the jangle of keys or the thud of a door. She even imagined it once—leapt up when she thought she heard a car door in the distance—but it had only been the wind catching the shutters. Her cheeks flushed in the quiet after, embarrassed, though no one had seen.

Nine passed. Then ten. The sound of the grandfather clock down the hall struck each hour like a gavel in judgment.

Alaric had come home late before—too many times for it to feel new. But he always came home. Tonight, the silence had a shape to it. A hollow.

She tried to read, but the words wouldn't stay still. They scattered the moment she reached for them, darting like minnows in a stream. Every time her eyes reached the bottom of a page, she realized she hadn't absorbed a single line.

She moved from chair to sofa and back again, fingers tugging at her skirt, ankles restlessly shifting. Her hands trembled once when she reached for the lamp to turn it off, but she didn't pull the chain. It felt wrong to darken the room before he returned.

And beneath it all, that creeping sense that this was her fault.

She had raised her voice. She had snapped. He'd tried to make it light again—offered her a smile—but she hadn't smiled back. Her words had been sharp enough to cut, and maybe they had.

So she rehearsed what she might say when he returned. "I was just tired." Or, "I didn't mean it." The words felt thin in her mouth, excuses more than truths. She tried them again, softer, but they didn't sound convincing—not to her.

She stayed in the sitting room, curled in a chair with her knees tucked beneath her, eyes fixed on the drive through the sheer curtains. Headlights never came. The door never opened. His voice never called to her.

Eventually, the guilt gave way to fatigue. When she finally slipped into sleep, it was without changing clothes,

without extinguishing the light. She still believed she
needed to be ready for when he arrived.

It was Lucille who found her.

Madison stirred at the soft knock, the creak of hinges,
the careful pause. The housekeeper's voice was always
cheerful, but now it sounded like fabric stretched too
tight—still whole, but close to tearing.

"Duchess?"

Lucille had seen her in all manner of states—sick, sulk-
ing, soaked from the garden—but never like this. Never
this fragile.

Madison sat up slowly. Her dress was wrinkled, the ribbon at her neck had come undone. Light was pouring in
too brightly for the hour she thought it was.

"Did he—?" she started to ask, but Lucille's look
stopped her.

Later that morning, she found her mother in the garden.

Vivienne was seated in her usual chair, dressed with care,
her lipstick precise. A tea tray had been brought out by
someone, but left untouched. The wineglass in her hand
was half-drained, her thumb circling the rim again and
again as though it might yield an answer.

Madison paused at the edge of the hedgerow. For a moment, Vivienne didn't look up. Her gaze rested on the roses, unfocused, as if she were searching past them for something she couldn't name. The flowers leaned in towards her like parishioners waiting for a benediction she had no strength to give.

"Mother," Madison said, her greeting soft but starched, like a pressed collar worn too tight.

Vivienne's eyes flicked toward her daughter, lingered just long enough to register something—weariness, maybe, or regret—before drifting back to the garden. She lifted the glass and took a slow sip, her wedding ring making a small, deliberate tap against the crystal. It sounded louder than it should have, like punctuation in a room without conversation.

Madison sat down opposite her, folding her hands neatly in her lap. The quiet stretched, filled only by the low hum of bees in the lavender and the occasional shift of branches in the breeze. Vivienne didn't move much—only the faint press of her lips against the rim, the shallow rise of her chest, as if even breathing required effort.

There was no mention of Alaric. No questions. Just the weight of something unspoken, settling between them heavier than the summer air. Madison studied her mother's face, searching for a crack, but Vivienne's expression remained carefully drawn—smooth, composed, with only a faint shadow beneath the eyes betraying that she hadn't slept.

Madison wondered if her mother's silence was because of guilt, or of worry, or something harder to name. But nothing revealed itself. Whatever lived behind her eyes stayed hidden.

Still, Madison didn't speak. She sat very straight in her chair, mirroring her mother's posture without meaning to, the hush between them deepening until it seemed part of the garden itself.

Somewhere in the house, a phone rang. Not nearby—muffled, distant, like a sound underwater. Both women turned their heads slightly, instinctively.

Vivienne didn't move. She just reached for her glass again.

Footsteps eventually followed, fast and uneven. Then Lucille's voice, tight and short of breath.

She stepped onto the garden path, eyes darting between them. Her hands were clenched at her sides, wringing the edge of her apron.

"They've found the boat," she said.

Vivienne's glass paused halfway to her lips.

Madison stood without realizing it.

No one spoke.

But the bees kept humming in the lavender—steady and indifferent.

CHAPTER TEN

The Mourning

No one dared weep.

The church was old stone, gray and grave in its silence. A familiar chapel reserved for Newport's most venerable families. Madison remembered being lifted onto those pews as a child, her father winking as he snuck her a peppermint during long sermons. Now, she felt diminished by the same space—pressed beneath its ceremonial weight. Sea air pressed gently through the stained-glass windows, carrying salt and incense in equal measure. Outside, white lilies bent in the breeze, heads bowed like mourners.

There was no body. Just the polished cherry wood casket resting at the altar, unfilled, untouched. It made grief feel suspended, unanchored.

They said recovery was impossible. The wreckage had been found, yes—but not Alaric. His ship had been dashed on the rocks up the coast, splintered like driftwood, the mast broken clean through.

The storm had been merciless, a sudden squall of violence that spoke of more than weather. It felt deliberate, familiar. A fit of rage that broke and vanished in the same breath, and when it stilled, he was gone. Only the deep knew where—and it wasn't speaking.

Alastair insisted on the service anyway. Closure, he called it—though his tone lacked conviction. The La Croix name did not retreat into quiet grief. It stood straight-backed in church pews, wore silence like a tailored suit, and let the world see only what was permitted. Even in death, appearances were everything. Especially in death.

Madison sat in the front row, clad in black, hands gloved and clasped in her lap. Her hat's veil trembled faintly with each breath. Beneath it, her face was stone—but she swallowed once, too hard.

Vivienne arrived late. She was elegant, of course—she always was—but the scent of wine clung to her, layered atop the lilac of her dress. She wore no hat. Her hair was immaculate, her face composed as always. Her eyes, however, had forgotten how to lie.

She sat beside Madison, as custom required—close enough to meet expectations, but not enough to offer comfort. Her hands folded neatly in her lap, as if cradling something fragile that might spill if touched.

The service began with a priest droning out the rites of passing with practiced solemnity. Madison heard none of it. Her ears roared with the pounding of her own heart. Her throat ached with the pressure of unshed tears. She tried to focus on the Scripture, the cadence of ritual, the comfort of tradition—but her mind kept slipping.

Was he really dead?

What if he wasn't? What if the storm had spared him—swept him to some forgotten shore from one of his own adventure tales, where he now lived beneath a foreign sun? What if, even now, he was making his way back to her, unaware of the grief he'd left in his wake?

She hated the questions. They felt childish. Weak. But they crept in all the same, trailing guilt like seaweed in the surf.

Lucille placed a steady hand on her shoulder. It said everything her mother wouldn't. Or couldn't. Madison couldn't react—her stillness was stitched into her dress. So, she sat taller, breathed slower, disappeared into herself. Her training—her upbringing—told her to endure. To mourn with dignity. To grieve without spectacle.

But inside, she was screaming.

After a hymn faded, a family-appointed speaker stepped forward—a cousin from Providence, stiff in posture, but smooth in tone. He spoke of legacy, of honor, of a life shaped by duty and salt air. Of a man born for the sea.

Madison listened, or tried to. The words were polished, careful. Unremarkable. They spoke of Alaric the patriarch, the businessman, the symbol. Not of Alaric the father.

Not of the man who once let her eat cake on the boat, insisting it was military rations. Who whistled off-key while tying his shoes. Who spun tales so vivid she could smell the air in them. Who sat beside her in the dark when she was frightened, and never once told her to be brave—just let her be small, and safe, and held.

The eulogy fell short. It read like something inscribed on the base of a forgotten statue, half-swallowed by ivy and time.

She blinked, throat tightening, and said nothing.

When the final hymn began, Madison rose with the rest of the congregation, her legs trembling beneath her. Her gloved hand reached for the pew to steady herself, but she stopped before she touched it. No. She would not falter. Not here. Not now.

She sang the words of the hymn without hearing her own voice. Her lips moved. Her posture was perfect. She was every inch a La Croix.

When the service ended, Alastair stood first—not to speak, just to walk. As if by custom alone, the family followed. One by one, they approached the altar to offer their final respects, most as empty as the casket. A nod. A gloved touch. A bowed head. A murmur of something too quiet to catch.

The mourners filtered out beneath the watchful eye of the waiting press, their whispers trailing like vapor in the wind. But Madison remained. She stepped forward alone, each movement composed, her heels echoing sharp and hollow against the marble.

She lingered for a while, staring down into the hollow space where a father should have been.

Then she leaned in.

And whispered in a voice so low that only the dead could hear:

"You should have stayed."

Then she turned and walked out into the cold Newport sun.

CHAPTER ELEVEN

The Doubt

The house had never felt so large.

After the funeral, the family returned to the manor in a hush. The staff moved quietly, with the restraint of those unsure whether to offer comfort or simply fade from sight. No one had eaten. The platters laid out in the dining room had been arranged hours earlier but remained untouched, like offerings at a shrine.

Vivienne sat by the tall windows of the drawing room, a glass of wine in her hand despite the hour. There was something faintly rebellious about the way she lounged. It wasn't grief that draped across her shoulders, not exactly. It was memory, and the weight of everything that had remained unspoken.

Madison sat beside her, their shoulders nearly touching but never quite meeting—like ships adrift on the same tide. Her hands rested in her lap, motionless. She said nothing.

Across the room, Beatrix La Croix, Alaric's sister, had only just arrived from overseas, the hem of her coat still dusted from the wind off the tarmac. Her entrance was as unannounced as it was unapologetic. She offered no embrace to Madison, only a curt nod to Alastair and a formal kiss to Vivienne. Then she settled into an armchair with the elegance of a woman who graced embassy halls and foreign salons.

From the hallway came a murmured exchange—Aunt Mattie's husband, Harrison, perhaps, or one of the cousins raised too properly to intrude. Their voices stayed out of sight, another layer of family presence without participation, as if grief came with assigned seating.

Alastair stood near the hearth, one hand tucked behind his back, the other occasionally flexing as if remembering how to grasp something long gone. His profile faced the unlit fireplace, but his gaze drifted above it, not truly landing anywhere. He looked like a statue carved from an older era—immovable, irrelevant, and cold to the touch.

It was Aunt Mattie who finally broke the silence. Her brooch catching the lamplight, her presence as commanding as ever. "Well," she said with her usual arched-brow candor, "is anyone planning to act like a human being today, or have we all been embalmed alongside that poor, empty box?"

Alastair gave no indication he heard her. Vivienne sipped her wine. Only Madison reacted, a small flicker of breath escaping her, like a sigh of relief.

Mattie's heels clicked as she crossed the floor. She circled behind them. "I hope you're proud." She placed a hand on the back of the chair between Madison and Vivienne and looked at no one in particular. "Alaric deserved more than this—this theatre of pretense and polished grief."

Vivienne's gaze didn't waver. "And what would you have us do, Matilda? We've buried a ghost."

"You didn't bury him. You buried doubt," Mattie snapped. "And I'd wager you're still clutching it like a rosary, hoping repetition will turn uncertainty into absolution."

Silence fell again, but heavier now. Madison felt it coil in her stomach. She had tried to stay composed, tried not to let the sadness win. But this wasn't sadness—it was the ache of absence; of a voice she'd never hear say her name again.

She stood politely. "Excuse me."

Mattie watched her go. Her expression softened, and for a moment she looked older than her years. "At least *she* still feels something," she murmured.

No one responded.

Outside, the sky over Newport hung grey and low. Madison walked to the far edge of the garden, where the sea met the cliffs in a sheer drop. The wind caught her hair, pulled at the hem of her coat. She didn't cry. She just stood there, letting the weight of everything settle over her, letting the silence speak in ways words never could.

She didn't hear the unusually soft tread behind her until it stopped just beside her. Aunt Mattie said nothing at first. She simply stood beside her, looking out across the sea as the waves broke against the cliffs below.

Then, gently—without a grand gesture or flourish—she moved and wrapped her arms around Madison from behind, resting her chin lightly atop Madison's head.

It wasn't how the women in their family embraced. It wasn't the sort of hug offered in condolence or sympathy. It was grounding, and whole, and steady. It felt warm and familiar, almost like her father.

Madison closed her eyes.

"I used to hold him like this," Mattie said quietly. "When he was small and didn't know how to be angry yet."

Madison didn't respond, but her breath hitched.

Mattie held her a little tighter. "You don't have to be strong in front of ghosts, darling. They already know who you are."

That did it. Her body didn't crumple, not all at once—but something inside her gave way. A sob forced its way out, sudden, like a thread pulled from a tightly woven seam. Then another. And another.

She turned into Mattie's arms and buried her face in her shoulder, no longer fighting the grief, no longer guarding herself from its weight. Her hands gripped at the older woman's coat, as though afraid she might disappear too.

The wind kept blowing, the cliffs stood steady, and the garden bore witness.

Mattie said nothing more. She just held her, steady as stone, and soft as a memory.

CHAPTER TWELVE

The Second Mourning

The house was empty again.

No longer the reverent hush of ceremony, but a silence that settles after something breaks. The mourners had gone, the flowers were already beginning to wilt in their vases. A few remained in the foyer—lilies and white roses, tired now, the water beneath them cloudy with rot.

Madison awoke before the staff had stirred. She didn't feel rested. Her limbs were leaden, her head thick.

The dress she had worn the day before still hung over the chair, black and solemn, its creases softened by sea air. The morning sun barely touched the lace curtains, its light hesitant, as if unsure it should intrude.

She shifted beneath the covers and froze. Something damp. Something wrong.

Lifting the sheets, she saw the stain—dark and blooming. Not the vivid red of scraped knees or childhood accidents. This was older, deeper. A kind of tired red, like rose petals pressed too long in a forgotten book.

Her breath caught. She sat upright and stared. No sound escaped her lips. No tears came. Just a stillness—rigid and numb—as she pulled her legs in and wrapped her arms around her knees.

At first, she thought she was dying. Not in the way a body fails, but in the way a heart does—suddenly, invisibly—until it starts leaking, too tired of holding everything in.

Her mind raced. She had read somewhere that grief could mimic illness—that sorrow could settle in the chest and press until it became something physical. Maybe this was that ache turned outward, visible at last. The body's attempt to make sense of something too enormous to handle.

Then she remembered a phrase—a whisper once overheard in the kitchen, or maybe from a cousin behind closed doors. She couldn't recall when, only the strange weight of it. "Becoming a woman."

There had been no preparation. No guidance. No warnings. Only blood and silence.

She peeled herself from the sheets and stood slowly, her movements stiff with uncertainty. A flush crept up her neck—not quite shame, but something close to it, cold and unfamiliar. Her nightgown clung to her thighs.

She wrapped the soiled linens into a ball, holding them away from her body, and slipped barefoot down the back stairs.

In the service corridor, the tile chilled her feet. She quietly turned the corner toward the laundry—but Lucille was already there, sorting towels. Lucille looked up, her expression shifting the moment she saw it. Her eyes softened. "Oh my sweet child."

Lucille stepped forward without a word, gently took the bundle from her arms, and set it aside in a basket.

Then she placed one steady hand on her cheek. "It's all right. It happens to all of us."

Madison didn't speak.

Lucille straightened and wrapped an arm around Madison's shoulders, guiding her a few steps down the hallway. "I'll bring you fresh linens," Lucille said lightly. "And something for the rest. Go wash up."

Madison nodded, barely, and turned back toward the stairs. The hallway stretched long and dim. Each step felt distant, like walking through someone else's memory. It was all a daze, like being underwater with no clear sense of direction, only the instinct to return to the surface.

She stepped back into her bedroom as if entering a different house—one where the air had thickened and everything familiar was missing. Her nightgown still stuck to her skin, an unwelcome, damp reminder of what had happened.

In the shower, she let the water run over her. It was warm, almost too warm, and she stood there for a long time, unmoving, as if the stream might dissolve what had just happened. She washed slowly, deliberately, like she was rinsing away something she couldn't name. Less of a cleansing, more of a ritual.

She grabbed a fresh gown from the wardrobe, moving slowly, like her limbs had forgotten how to work together. She sat on the edge of the bed for a long moment, hands resting in her lap, staring at the floor without really seeing it.

When Lucille arrived, she gave her a discreet package wrapped in brown paper and tucked it into her hands with a reassuring smile. She set the clean white linens neatly on the nearby chair and gave Madison's hand a gentle squeeze. "I'll be back shortly to help you with everything," she said softly, her tone more comfort than instruction.

After a moment, Madison stood up. She remade the bed herself. Folded the black dress and carefully set it back on its hanger. Then she lay on the clean white sheets, arms crossed over her chest and stared up at the ceiling.

Outside, the sound of the waves roared on, unbothered, like the family who had just gathered at her father's funeral. Present, composed, and untouched by the weight of what had been lost.

Her childhood was being buried. No casket. Not even a eulogy.

CHAPTER THIRTEEN

The Memorial

The air hung with catering and ceremony.

The lawn had been raked into perfection, but the roots still buckled beneath the sod. Hydrangeas burst too eagerly along the edges—blue as bruises—while white canvas tents fluttered in the coastal wind like sails.

It had been a year since Alaric's funeral. In that time, Vivienne had begun work on what would become Resonance—a cultural initiative centered on music and the arts. It promised scholarships, instruction, and expression for those without the luxury of any of them. Whether it was genuinely meant to honor his memory or merely an attempt to carve a more permanent place for Vivienne, Madison wasn't sure.

She stood two paces behind her mother, positioned carefully for the press. Her chin was tilted just enough to suggest interest but not engagement, a look she had learned by watching older women at family galas—elegance as a form of absence.

The podium bore a modest brass plaque:

Resonance: In Memory of Alaric La Croix

The "La Croix" had been etched more deeply than the rest, as though someone had gone over it twice.

Vivienne's voice hovered above the small crowd, light and lilting; her accent more refined today than usual. "Music has always had a way of reaching into places where words cannot tread. When I lost my husband—when *we* lost him—there were days when the only thing that could carry me forward was the sound of a cello in the other room... or the scratch of a record."

Madison didn't flinch, though she felt the shift. The turn of phrase. Her mother hadn't played a record in years, and no one Madison knew played the cello. She made no mention of the piano either—the one Madison played until her hands began to tremble.

A gentle applause followed. One of the city council members even dabbed his eye with a handkerchief. A seagull cried overhead, louder than the clapping.

Behind the performance stood the building that would house Resonance—an old seaside estate with its windows reglazed and halls freshly painted. A local artist had filled the north wall with a mural, something vaguely symbolic and full of color. Inside, the rooms had been repurposed for violin lessons, creative writing workshops, and week-ly recitals. The grandeur of its architecture still lingered beneath the renovation, like a memory too proud to be painted over.

It was, by every outward measure, a lovely thing. And still—Madison felt herself folding in against it. Not in protest. In preservation—holding her father's memory as her own, safe from the way her mother dressed it.

When the speech ended, Madison watched Vivienne step down in soft heels and accept the delicate grip of a socialite who used to sit beside her at luncheons, their exchange choreographed for cameras and self-congratula-tion. Reporters pressed in with scripted urgency, asking prepared questions they already knew the answers to.

Behind them, champagne glasses clinked, and a pho-tographer directed two city officials to stand closer to the La Croix crest etched into the mural wall. Everything was being preserved—on paper, on film, and in the minds of those who needed to be seen.

Madison, meanwhile, drifted.

She stepped off the edge of the tented clearing, away from the applauding circle, down the path toward the back of the old building. The stone underfoot was sun-warmed, flaked in salt.

Past the side garden, down a narrow gravel slope, she found a shaded terrace where the formality gave way to age. The paths here weren't overgrown, just forgotten. A stone bench leaned against the wall, and ivy crept over the base like a shawl drawn in for comfort.

She kept walking.

There was no aim to it—just the instinct to be elsewhere. To distance herself from all the pretense. She followed a footpath that bent behind a grove of trees, then past the remains of a rusted trellis. The world grew quieter with each step.

And then—a sound. Not the distant chatter of applause, but something closer. A sharp clearing of the throat, nerveless and real, cutting across the hush of the garden like a pebble dropped into still water.

She froze.

Beneath the shade of a half-dead willow sat a boy about her age with a book open in his lap, fully absorbed. The title, she recognized, was one of her favorites.

He had a shock of dark hair that fell toward his brow, the same black-blue shade that used to catch light in her father's photographs. His clothes were clean but slightly worn—his collar curled at the edges, his cuffs a little frayed. The shoes were too big, likely handed down. And still, there was something familiar in the way he sat—shoulders relaxed, back straight.

She watched the way his eyes moved across the page—focused, deliberate, too engrossed to notice her. He would sometimes pause and glance upward as if picturing something, then return to the words with renewed certainty. He didn't skip or skim, didn't rush.

She didn't mean to linger but found herself rooted. The book, the mannerisms, the dark hair—all of it drew her in like a ghost she did not believe in but couldn't look away from. Her chest tightened, just slightly.

Suddenly, the sound of distant clapping called her back to reality, like a bell rung at the end of something sacred. Her legs obeyed before her heart did. She turned, slowly, as if pulling free from a dream, and walked reluctantly back towards the main building.

Her mother was assembling the family for the final photo—an image destined for society pages and charity galas, curated not just to mark the end of an era but to prove, on glossy paper, that the La Croix's endured. A commemoration of legacy, yes—but also of absence, of a man whose shadow still outshone the room.

Madison arrived just in time.

CHAPTER FOURTEEN

The Friendship

Madison had been waiting patiently.

The speeches had faded into memory, the ribbon long since cut, but today—Resonance's first true recital—still shimmered with lights and lenses. It had been an orchestrated event. Music students performed, donors clapped, and Vivienne offered poised praise about youth, art, and opportunity.

Madison hadn't said a word. She didn't need to. Her presence was the proof of her support. The La Croix legacy on display. A symbol. And everyone knew it.

She stood in the back hallway of the building, still in her polished dress and borrowed smile, listening to her mother's laughter drift out from the reception room. She waited for a lull—just long enough for the photographers to turn toward the stage again—then slipped off her heels and padded quietly toward the rear exit.

The hallway smelled faintly of polish and perfume, but outside, the evening met her with damp stone and wind. No one saw her exit. Or if they did, they said nothing.

Outside, the garden had taken root, and the salt air made even the dirt smell alive. She cut through the low hedges and toward the far edge of the lot, where an old stone wall marked the boundary between the center and the neglected lot next door.

He was there.

Same dark curls. A different book—the spine bent from rereading, the cover rubbed soft at the corners. He turned pages slowly, half reading, half watching the dimming sky. His shirt hung untucked, collar loose, fingers drumming the bench in a rhythm too sharp to be careless. It had the twitch of someone impatient, like he was waiting for something—or someone.

His name was Eli. He didn't speak much about himself, but Madison felt she knew him anyway—through the things he read, the lines he lingered over. It was enough.

He didn't notice her approach until she cleared her throat.

"You always read the good ones twice?"

He looked up and smiled without hesitation. "Only the ones that get better when you already know the ending."

She sat beside him on the cool stone, tucking her dress beneath her. "That's a good rule."

"What about you? Still sneaking out of important things?"

"I *am* the important thing," she said flatly, then let the joke breathe between them. Eli laughed, and she let herself smile—really smile—for the first time in days.

She had been sneaking out for weeks—slipping away between her assigned volunteer shifts at Resonance, kids' piano lessons or ushering in the recital room. She was expected to be useful, present, and refined. But once the last chairs were straightened and the donors turned their eyes elsewhere, she vanished. And no one noticed.

It was the only part of Resonance that felt real to her. The rest—the careful smile, the practiced nod, the poise that made adults proud—felt like a costume she couldn't take off. But this? This was something different. It made the rest worth enduring. Here, behind the building, with dirt beneath her toes and no one watching, Madison felt like she could be herself.

They mostly talked about books—the ones that stayed with you, like a tune you couldn't shake. The ones they'd hidden in drawers or given away just to stop thinking about them. They joked about overrated authors and made a quiet list of the ones who felt like friends. Madison said she liked strong characters who knew what they wanted—and didn't apologize for it. Eli said he liked the ones who dove headfirst into danger and figured it out along the way.

Sometimes they talked about movies—the ones based on books they both knew by heart. He groaned about endings that were changed for no reason and made no sense. She rattled off every plot hole the adaptation had invented. They argued about casting choices—who looked right, who didn't, and whether it ever mattered as much as the words they left out.

They made up their own stories—usually about the archaic building that lurked behind them. She said the cracked pavement behind it was once a secret stage, where lanterns lit midnight plays. He countered that it was where the props were burned afterward, so no one could ever perform them again. The broken gutter, she guessed, might be hiding something valuable—coins dropped by careless hands. He smirked and said it probably held a knife, left to rust until the rain washed the handle away.

When the breeze picked up, she pulled her skirt tighter around her knees. He raised an eyebrow and offered his jacket with exaggerated formality, one arm draped like a butler. "Milady," he said with a grin.

"You'd miss it too much," she replied, waving it off. He clutched it to his chest as if wounded, then staggered back dramatically and collapsed onto the grass with a groan. "Tell my story," he said faintly, eyes closed. She rolled her eyes and flicked a pebble at his shoulder. She didn't mind the performance. It just made her smile.

It wasn't serious. It wasn't that deep. But it was theirs, and it made her world feel lighter, less bound by rules.

Eventually, the sun dipped, shadows stretching long across the grass—like the docks at the end of a sail, borrowed time slipping away.

Reluctantly, she stood. "Same time next week?"

He looked up, squinting. "You make the rules, remember?"

"No," she said. "I don't... at least not here."

Here there was no curation. No schedule. No expectations. And for once, she didn't know the ending—at least not yet.

And that was why she came back.

CHAPTER FIFTEEN

The Edge of Want

M adison always anticipated their time.

The garden had grown over since spring, green bleeding into the stone path. But it had become their place—quiet, shaded, tucked away from everything that demanded too much. Eli was already there when Madison arrived, sitting cross-legged, a book half-open beside him, as though the story could only move forward once she appeared.

It wasn't on any schedule, but it had become its own kind of appointment. A pause in everything else. She liked that he always waited but never said it aloud. Their rhythm had become familiar. Predictable. Comfortable.

Until it wasn't.

The change wasn't loud. Not a thunderclap, but a pressure — like the air shifting before a storm. Madison felt it right away. She didn't know what had changed, exact-ly—just that something had begun to move in the wrong direction.

They were laughing. About something dumb—about the way a character in a book said "darling" too much. Eli laughed with her, but then the sound thinned. A pause stretched, holding something back.

That's when she saw him looking at her. *Really* looking.

Not the casual glance, not the quick grin. This was different. His eyes lingered—steady, deliberate. Not curious. Not amused. Searching. Consuming.

He shifted closer. Just a little. Close enough to change the air between them, close enough that her next breath caught before she could stop it.

His fingers brushed hers—it wasn't an accident.

He hesitated, then said it—softly, carefully, like testing a door he wasn't sure was unlocked: "You're really pretty."

The words landed heavy. Madison blinked. For a moment, she didn't move. Heat rose up her neck, not flattery but unease, sharp and sudden. She looked at him, not unkindly, but with the sudden clarity of someone realizing she'd grown too careless with someone she barely knew.

She drew her hand back—not abruptly, not rudely. But enough. A clear refusal without words.

He looked embarrassed. Mumbled something. Said it was nothing.

But it wasn't nothing.

He lowered his eyes, ashamed, and slowly shifted back, his movements careful and steady. He retreated to a safer distance, as if space alone could undo what had just transpired.

Afterward, they sat in silence, the air between them filled with words neither of them could say. When she finally stood, he didn't stop her.

She walked back to the building alone, the sound of her own footsteps louder than usual on the stone path. No goodbye. No explanation.

For a moment, she almost stopped. Almost turned back, almost said something. But what?

So, she kept walking, slow and deliberate, like a book set down — unfinished.

That night, Madison couldn't sleep. The room was too quiet. Her pillow was too warm. The sheets were too tight. She kept thinking—not about him, but about herself.

She had been dreaming—chasing the echo of her father. Her mother was living her own dream with Resonance, polished, public, and pretentious. Madison's version had been quieter, hidden, but just as false. But now the spell was broken, and it was gone.

She had mistaken comfort for safety, lost herself in wanting what wasn't there. That was the part she couldn't forgive—the naivety, the carelessness of it.

Lying there in the dark, something in her shifted. She didn't yet know what it meant.

But the part of her that trusted too easily, who slipped
so willingly into dreaming—
was gone.

CHAPTER SIXTEEN

The Rumor

There were always three of them.

Lydia Montgomery, radiant and magnetic, had always drawn attention like a lit match in a darkened room. Her laughter rang too loud in the dining hall, her stories inflated just enough to make the girls lean in. She chased the spotlight with both desperation and entitlement. Like it was her birthright. Her beauty was effortless, her performance was honed. Madison saw it now—not just the effect, but the hunger underneath. Lydia wanted to be seen. Not just noticed—admired. Revered. She needed eyes on her to feel real.

Abigail Dunn, in contrast, moved like ambition in a blazer. She was never loud, never crude, but consistently correct. She always had tissues, gum, and an answer—even if no one asked for it. Her smarts were like a shield—polished, and a boundary between her and everything else. Abigail didn't want to be seen in the same way Lydia did. She wanted to be acknowledged. She wanted to be right. Being right meant control, and control meant safety. Madison understood that better than either of them.

And Madison? She wore restraint like a second skin—not to impress, but to disappear into a shape no one could challenge. Her posture was perfect, her voice measured, her uniform tailored to suggest taste, never rebellion. She didn't chase admiration or correctness—she curated them. Every expression was chosen, every silence deliberate. Because if she was flawless, she couldn't be blamed. If she gave nothing away, nothing could be taken. Properness wasn't a performance; it was a fortress.

Around her, the other girls slipped themselves into every moment—every conversation, every glance. They were governed by their emotions, even as they pretended otherwise. It was as if they were all rehearsing what they saw at home, practicing the same performance of their parents in miniature. Gossip was still traded, alliances still shifted, laughter still cut. Smaller, softer, but no less familiar.

It wasn't that Madison was above it, though sometimes it felt that way. She simply spoke less. Listened more. Saw more.

In their trio, she wasn't the loudest or the most insistent. But she was the one they looked to when something shifted—when a response was needed, or when silence carried more weight than words.

Without ever asking for it, Madison had become the axis they spun around.

The rumor arrived before the first bell.

Whispers flickered through the halls like smoke, impossible to trace. A kiss, a moonlit meeting with somebody from the boys' school. None of it confirmed. But it all pointed toward someone—anyone. The mystery was the allure.

By recess, it had taken hold. Girls clutched books they weren't reading—their knuckles white against the spine. They leaned together in tight clusters, each glance a silent accusation. A quiet question hung in the air: Who was it?

Lydia turned to the others, flushed and breathless, oscillating between faux innocence and giddy delight. "Do you think they believe it's me?" she asked more than once, eyes hopeful, lips bitten pink. She loved scandal, until she didn't—when the glances turned judgmental, and teachers called her aside.

Abigail stiffened at once, outraged not by the content but by the inaccuracy. "The entire thing is ridiculous." She began constructing her case like a lawyer, listing plausibility, inaccurate timelines, and lack of motives.

And Madison? She just blinked, shrugged, and took a sip of her water bottle.

At lunch, a swarm of girls descended on their table—giggling, bold with secondhand gossip. "We heard it might be one of you," one said, grinning like the game was afoot.

Lydia laughed coyly, fingers brushing the ribbons in her hair as if drawing attention to them. Abigail looked irritated, adjusting her glasses with a sharp push of one finger. Madison just tilted her head, eyes calm and unreadable.

"If it were," she said slowly, "why would we tell you?"

It wasn't said with malice. It was just true.

The swarm faltered, disappointed by the lack of reaction—by the calm, disinterested dismissal. They lingered for a breath, then drifted away in search of easier prey.

Lydia and Abigail exchanged a glance once the girls were gone. Lydia leaned in with a conspiratorial grin, cheeks still flushed. "That was perfect," she whispered, half in awe. Abigail allowed herself a rare smile, smoothing her skirt. "I do love when they leave confused." Madison didn't respond. She simply picked up her fork and returned to her lunch.

Between classes, a bold girl came up to them on a mission. She outright asked if it was Madison, with the kind of voice that carried just enough to be overheard by the other girls in the hallway.

Lydia gave a nervous laugh, too bright to be casual. Abigail bristled beside her, already forming the rebuttal Madison refused to give. Madison looked at her for a moment before shutting her locker.

"People believe what they want," she said simply, then turned to walk back to class without waiting for a reply. Lydia and Abigail fell in step behind her—Abigail steady, Lydia smirking as they passed the girl still standing there, unsure what had just happened.

By the end of the day, the attention had moved on. Lydia's reputation was slightly bruised, Abigail's mood was frayed. But Madison remained untouched.

She hadn't started the rumor. But she saw how it gripped them—all of them, in glances and whispers and breathless guesses. And she remained on the edge of it all.

Later, in the slow crawl of cars outside St. Catherine's, Madison sat back in the seat. Her gaze drifted past the side window. Her thoughts circled back to Eli—the boy behind Resonance. How they had slipped away and stayed until dusk, the outside lamps buzzing to life against the half-light.

Had anyone seen them?

For a moment, beneath all her composure, a quiet doubt unsettled her.

Maybe the rumor really was about her.

CHAPTER SEVENTEEN

The Lost Legacy

The magazine slid across the cafeteria table without a word.

Abigail didn't meet Madison's eyes—just tapped the glossy cover once with her fingernail and returned to her sandwich. On the cover: a sepia-toned photo of Alaric La Croix at the helm of his beloved yacht. Below it, in bold serif font: *"Mystery at Sea: The Lost Legacy of Alaric La Croix."*

Madison's fingers landed gently on the edge, but the stillness of her hand betrayed nothing. Inside, though, she felt it—that low pulse of something colder than fear. She slipped the magazine into her satchel with practiced ease, folding herself back into the conversation as if nothing had happened.

Later that evening, in the quiet of her room, she read it.

The article was well crafted. A double-page spread of archival photographs led into a long-form narrative filled with veiled conjecture. It began with soft reverence— "a man of the sea," "scion of Newport"—but the tone sharpened by paragraph three. There were no direct accusations, only questions. But they were the kind that left marks:

> Despite official closure, the wreckage, including the body, was never fully recovered. Sources close to the investigation recall discrepancies in reported times and final transmissions.

> A once-public man who became increasingly withdrawn. Some say he was carrying the burden of more than just the family business.

> When asked about her late husband, Vivienne La Croix offered this: 'Alaric was impossible in all the ways that make a man unforgettable. But when he loved you—even for a moment—you felt like the only person

in the world. I suppose that was his gift... and
his curse.'

Madison read her mother's quote three times before
realizing her eyes were moving. It repeated itself in her
mind long after she set the magazine down.

And on the last page, there it was. Something buried at
the end of the article, like a treasure waiting to be found.

A photograph Madison hadn't seen in years. She was
younger then, posed beside her father on the dock in a
linen dress, eyes wide beneath a sunhat too large for her
head. Madison had forgotten how small she looked next
to him.

The caption read like something out of a eulogy:

> A delicate flower at the edge of lega-
> cy—Madison La Croix, pictured with her fa-
> ther during their final summer together.

It cast her as something innocent. Untouched. Fragile.
As if she were a petal clinging to a stem, tumbling through
the air on its way to the sea.

Alastair, of course, had declined to comment. The article noted that tersely, as if his silence were a clue in itself.
But Vivienne had spoken. Spoken with polish. With precision. With the ease of someone who knew exactly which
truths to leave out. Just enough ambiguity to keep the
scent of scandal alive.

At school, the article was fuel.

The girls discussed it in careless whispers—at lockers, in the restroom, even during morning announcements. They shared rumors like secrets, each retelling more dramatic than the last, as if proximity to tragedy might rub off on them somehow.

"It's kind of romantic, don't you think?" someone said. "Like, dying with your ship?"

"I heard there were drugs on board."

"I heard there was another woman with him. That he was having an affair."

"No way—he killed himself. You don't just crash like that by accident."

Madison heard it all. She didn't respond. She let it wash over her.

But it was harder this time. Looks followed her through the halls—no longer sharp or gleeful, but softened, uncertain. Girls didn't whisper now; they just stared for a second too long before pretending they hadn't. It wasn't the cruelty of scandal anymore. It was sympathy. Pity. And that was worse.

She kept her head high, movements smooth, her silence intact. But inside, something buckled by the weight of attention that was unbearable.

In the quiet that followed, she noticed something. The girls at school whispered to feel special—dropping hints and glances, hoping someone would pick up the pieces and ask them for more.

The adults whispered for different reasons. They re-shaped the truth to feel justified.

That night, Madison sat by her window, watching the wind stir the oaks that lined the edge of the La Croix estate. The magazine sat folded on her desk, the corner curling upward like it was trying to speak again.

She hadn't thrown it out. Lucille had offered, even held out her hands for it, like someone bracing to catch a crystal vase.

But Madison said no.

She had worked so hard to put him behind her. Not to forget—she never could—but to box up the grief, seal it in something clean, orderly, quiet. To let the ache of his absence become a part of the furniture of her life. For three years, she'd rehearsed the silence, folded it into ritual, into routine.

But this... this tore the lid off.

Madison looked out her window toward the dark horizon, where the sea met the sky in an indistinct blur. For a moment, she could almost see it—her father's boat, small and white against the blue-gray vastness, cutting silently across the water. But no matter how hard she strained her eyes, it refused to appear.

The moment dissolved like mist, and the questions from the article returned. Not the idle ones traded in hallways and lunchrooms. These were older, sharper—the kind she carried late at night, wondering if the sea had taken him clean, or if there was more to it. More than anyone dared say aloud.

But the article had dared. And it hadn't just asked questions—it provided revisions. It rewrote the dead.

And Madison wasn't sure if her mother had handed them the pen.

CHAPTER EIGHTEEN

The Confrontation

A breeze nudged the curtains like someone about to enter.

Madison descended the staircase, hearing the soft clink of porcelain and the sound of a page turning. Breakfast at home with her mother had become a ritual of shared silence, a quiet coexistence.

Vivienne sat at the breakfast table, a cup of black coffee beside her. Her eyes were fixed on the glossy spread of a magazine. The headline was unmistakable even from a distance: *"Mystery at Sea: The Lost Legacy of Alaric La Croix."*

Madison froze momentarily, feeling a chill wrap around her spine. Seeing it here, out in the open, felt disturbingly personal. Her mother looked up, noticing Madison's hesitation at the doorway. Vivienne's face stayed calm, but her eyes were less difficult to read. There was something beneath them—vulnerability.

"Are you happy with it?" Madison asked. She hadn't meant it to sound so harsh, but the words just came out. The question hung suspended between them, heavy and charged.

Vivienne folded the magazine slowly, deliberately, her slender fingers precise. She sighed, setting the magazine aside. "Happy? No. But I expected it. People always want answers—even if they have to make them up."

Madison slid into the seat across from her. The room felt different today—like it was waiting for something. As if the table itself had been set for confrontation.

"Are any of them true?" she asked.

Vivienne's eyes softened, glancing down, tracing the intricate edge of the lace tablecloth with her fingertip. "Some truths are harder than others, Madison. The truth is that your father was complicated. He had secrets. But not all secrets are sinister."

"Then why does everyone make them sound that way?" Madison asked tentatively, her initial edge fading into genuine curiosity, wanting—perhaps for the first time—to truly hear her mother's answer.

Vivienne met her daughter's eyes steadily. "Because scandal sells, my dear. And because people need villains—especially in stories they can't explain."

Madison hesitated.

She watched her mother's hands. Vivienne fidgeted with things when she didn't know what to say. She'd tap her fingers on her cup, fold and refold her napkin, move the saltshaker back and forth. It reminded Madison of someone stalling for time—like she was trying to figure out the right move but didn't want to show her hand.

"Did you hate him?" The question came out before Madison could stop it. She hadn't planned to say it. But the question had lingered, unspoken for years.

Vivienne laughed, bitter and brittle, like glass underfoot. "Hate? No. Never hate." She shook her head, slowly. "But resentment... perhaps. Your father had a gift for drawing people close, then pulling away." She paused for a breath, looking out the window as if she was watching him out on the lawn. "Even from me."

The silence after lingered, heavy with things neither had ever said aloud before. For the first time she could remember, Madison saw something in her mother beyond resentment—maybe regret, even sadness.

Vivienne traced the rim of her cup, voice quieter now. "You know, Madison. You have something I never did. You're a La Croix. You walk into a room and they all hush."

Madison didn't respond at first. She thought back to the spring gala—how everyone had looked at her mother, but then their eyes started to shift. Slowly. Until she could feel them on her, too. Like something settling over her shoulders.

Madison's eyes wavered, offering something close to grace. "You are, too."

Her mother's expression shifted, her smile tilted with a kind of practiced glamour. Maybe it was envy. Or even recognition. "Oh, I wear the name like a gown I borrowed for the evening. Beautiful, sure, but not really mine. You... you were born with it. It fits like your skin."

For a fleeting moment, Madison glimpsed a reflection of herself in Vivienne's eyes—both of them bound by invisible threads of expectation and longing.

"It's not that simple," Madison whispered.

"No," Vivienne agreed, drawing a slow breath, steadying herself. "Nothing in this family ever is."

As they sat quietly, an uneasy peace settled between the soft clink of silver and the shifting morning light. For the first time, Madison felt something like understanding pass between them—fragile, delicate, easily shattered.

For now, it was enough.

CHAPTER NINETEEN

The Academy

It almost felt cruel.

The transition from St. Catherine's girls school to Ashmore Academy, a co-ed institution with manicured grounds and a long history of tradition, had promised prestige. What it delivered was confusion.

Madison noticed it in small ways—the way conversations faltered, the way glances lingered a second too long. There was a new currency in the air, something unspoken but as thick as humidity.

Power hierarchies were starting to form, and students were being sorted in subtle ways. In classrooms, it was how you asked a question—or if you dared to answer one. Whether your voice carried confidence or caution. Clubs became arenas of soft politics: debate, theatre, student council. Even the hallways told a story—who moved in tight clusters, who trailed behind. Everything meant something. Everything was a signal.

Friendships shifted, not out of betrayal but realignment. The social map redrew itself week by week, cliques forming and reforming like shoals of fish in unfamiliar water.

But through it all, there remained the three of them—Madison, Lydia, and Abigail. One of the few constants in a school learning how to see itself anew.

For Lydia, Ashmore was heaven. She had matured over the summer, curves arriving with the confidence of someone who had always expected them. Her skirts pushed the edge of what was allowed, and her blouses were just tight enough to earn double takes. She spoke louder now, laughed even more deliberately. Her power was immediate and direct.

For Abigail, it was the opposite. She had filled out more than she wanted to, in ways that brought attention she hadn't asked for. In protest, she wore oversized sweaters, sleeves pulled over her hands, posture slumped inwards as if to fold herself smaller. She was always scanning the hallway, always bracing.

Madison, too, had changed. She was taller, more refined—but she wore her uniform with a kind of studied restraint. A fitted blazer, clean lines, everything pressed and perfect. She didn't need to rebel with her hemline. She commanded with poise.

The boys didn't know what to do with the three of them. Their eyes followed them down the corridor, unsure whether to flirt, impress, or steer clear. The trio seemed to walk in sync without trying, and the silence they left in their wake said more than any gossip could.

And Madison saw them watching. All of them.

The cafeteria was its own ecosystem—equal parts stage and courtroom. Seniors had long claimed the center tables by the windows and glass-paneled courtyard. Juniors flanked them, orbiting the prime real estate with practiced deference. The underclassmen were still learning the rules. They watched and mimicked—sitting too close one day, too far the next—constantly recalibrating.

Madison, Lydia, and Abigail had claimed a table on the outer edge of the courtyard zone. Not too forward, not invisible. It was just enough to be noticed without seeming to ask for it. Others joined sometimes—girls from their year, mostly—but none stayed long. The balance was delicate.

One day, a new girl lingered near their table. She was pale, dark-haired, and small, with a backpack that still had the creases from shipping. Her uniform hung awkwardly—slightly too loose at the shoulders, the blazer bunching where it should taper. Her eyes scanned the cafeteria in cautious sweeps before settling on their table—the only one with just enough space left to be plausible.

She hesitated.

Lydia and Abigail noticed her at the same time. They didn't say a word, just turned slightly—shoulders angled, expressions neutral—waiting for Madison's response.

Madison didn't balk. She gestured to the empty spot. "You can sit here."

The girl exhaled a sigh of relief. "Thanks," she mumbled, sliding in quickly and introducing herself as Nina. Her voice was soft.

Madison studied her. After a few moments of silence, she spoke. "Are you new here?"

Nina looked up, surprised to be asked. "Yeah. I just transferred. From... Uh... Grant High."

"Where's that?" Abigail asked, her brows knitting slightly as if irritated by the gap in her knowledge.

"Jersey," Nina said. She paused, then added, "It was a public school."

"Public school?" Lydia said, her tone shifting slightly, just short of patronizing. "That's... different. What made you come here?"

Nina hesitated. Her fingers curled around the edge of the table instead, eyes dropping for a moment. Then, more quietly than before, she said, "I got a scholarship."

"A scholarship?" Abigail repeated, like she was trying out the word. Then she added, "That's impressive."

Nina gave a weak laugh, a little embarrassed. "Yeah... it's a lot." She looked down again, then added, almost automatically, "My mom says it'll be worth it."

Madison gave the faintest smile—just enough to regis-ter. She wasn't judging. She was curious. She couldn't remember the last time somebody had credited their mother for a decision.

"Well, Ashmore's different," Madison said lightly. "But I'm sure you'll figure it out."

Nina gave a small smile, then unwrapped her sandwich—a plain-looking thing on soft white bread—and began to eat quietly.

Madison watched Nina for a moment longer. There was a stiffness in the girl's shoulders, a way she held herself like she was waiting to be dismissed. She was neither defiant nor hopeful. Just holding her breath in case she needed to disappear.

Madison went back to her own lunch.

But the table felt different with four.

CHAPTER TWENTY

The Story

Ashmore's library had the scent of old paper and worn floorboards, and the kind of calm that made thoughts feel heavier—more private. Madison liked it there. Not just for the quiet, but also the sense of order. Shelves labeled in gold script. Everything in its place. It was grounding.

She was halfway through outlining an English paper when she noticed Nina again—two tables over, backpack tucked at her feet, scribbling in a spiral notebook with an expression that was oddly intense. Her brow furrowed one second, then lifted in satisfaction the next, as if whatever she was writing had finally landed right.

Madison stood and wandered closer. "What are you working on?"

Nina looked up, surprised but not displeased. "A first draft. For creative writing. We got to pick anything. I'm doing a story about this girl who discovers she can reshape reality just by writing it down."

Madison tilted her head. "That sounds... better than anything I've come up with."

Nina gave a modest shrug. "It just came out fast, I guess. Sometimes they do. I've always loved making up stories."

Madison pulled out a chair. "My dad used to tell stories like that. All kinds—funny ones, spooky ones, even the kind that didn't make much sense but felt good anyway. I used to love just listening to him talk."

There was a pause—brief, but sharp. Nina's expression faltered. She nodded slowly and looked down.

Madison caught it. She didn't push.

They sat for a moment, the silence stretching. Then Madison glanced at Nina's notebook. "You don't use cursive?"

Nina shook her head. "I never really learned. I just write in print. It's slower, but I don't mind."

"Doesn't that take forever?"

Nina smiled faintly. "Probably. But it's easier to read."

There was something matter-of-fact in the way Nina said it. No embarrassment. Just the truth.

Nina's eyes drifted across the table. "That's a really nice pen," she said. "Is it yours?"

Madison glanced down. It was one that Lucille had placed in her backpack. Sleek, gold-capped, absurdly smooth. "Yeah," she said, almost apologetically.

Nina gave a little nod. "It just looks... really nice. Was it a gift? It looks like the kind of thing you get for something important."

Madison didn't quite know how to respond. She thought of the drawer full of them at home. They were nothing close to special.

She shifted slightly. "You know, Resonance has writing programs. Creative nonfiction, poetry, narrative. You might like it."

Nina looked at her, cautious. "What's Resonance?"

"It's this program my mom started. For music and writing and stuff. Kind of like a community thing," Madison said.

"It's for students of Ashmore?"

"It's for anyone who wants to learn something," Madison said. "They do workshops after school and on the weekends. You'd probably enjoy it."

Madison rarely mentioned Resonance unless she had to. It always felt like one of those things her mother used to be seen doing something generous. She hadn't planned to bring it up now—it just slipped out, maybe because Nina actually seemed like she'd benefit from it. Or maybe because, for once, Madison wanted it to mean something more than optics.

Nina hesitated. "Would my mom be able to come?"

Madison blinked. "To... the workshop?"

Nina flushed a little. "Just wondering. In case she had to wait."

Madison studied her. That wasn't how things worked in her world. Not even close.

"Yeah, I guess," she said after a pause.

Nina looked almost relieved. Then curious. "Do you go to Resonance?"

The question caught Madison off guard. She opened her mouth, then closed it again. "Me? I mean… yeah, but just to help out. It's more my mom's thing."

Nina nodded. "Maybe I'll see you there then."

"Yeah, maybe," Madison said, the words automatic, her mind already turning over what that would even look like.

Nina smiled and went back to her notebook, pencil moving with deliberate purpose.

Madison stood, gathering her things. She didn't say goodbye, but she glanced back once as she left. Nina didn't see her. She looked like she was already off on some adventure of her own, half-smiling, lost in thought.

Nina wasn't like most of Madison's friends. There was something softer in her—childlike, almost. It was kind of endearing. And a little worrying, too. The world, and especially Ashmore, didn't go easy on people like that.

She'd need to grow up fast.

CHAPTER TWENTY-ONE

The Finalist

Resonance always looked different in daylight.

The music rooms were tucked behind frosted glass, and the writing lounge had windows that caught the afternoon sun just enough to feel warm but not intrusive. Someone had left a bowl of clementines by the sign-in sheet. The scent lingered faintly in the air, citrusy and clean.

Nina paused at the threshold like she didn't want to interrupt anything, then offered a small, shy wave to the receptionist. Her clothes were neat, her backpack carefully zipped—as if she was trying to do everything right without being told how. But her face lit up when she saw the space: soft chairs, empty notebooks, colored pens. Freedom.

The workshop instructor was named Molly. Late twenties, maybe. A graduate student with paint on her jeans and a string of mismatched bracelets up one arm. She didn't perform kindness—she just lived in it. No forced smiles. No pageant voice. When she asked Nina if she'd been to a workshop before and Nina shook her head, Molly just grinned and said, "Good. No habits to break."

That first session, Nina hardly spoke. But she wrote like she'd been waiting for someone to ask. Madison didn't sit in, but she lingered just long enough to see Molly kneel beside Nina's chair, read a few lines, and laugh in the most natural way.

By the third week, Nina was helping lead the opening warm-up. She didn't realize it, not exactly, but she was good. The kind of good that didn't have to be loud. Molly asked her to read one of her pieces aloud. Nina hesitated. Then nodded.

The story was short—only a few paragraphs—but it hummed. It was about a girl who found a locked garden and imagined it into bloom, describing every petal and stem until something began to grow. Molly really liked it.

After the session, Molly mentioned a national youth fiction contest she'd been looking at, one that could really open doors for Nina. "I've been waiting for the right piece," she said. "I think this could be the one. Would you be willing to expand it a little? Flesh it out before I send it in?"

Nina looked stunned. "I didn't write it for that."

"That's why it works," Molly said.

Nina hesitated, then nodded. Molly beamed.

Two weeks later, Nina was named a finalist. Molly made the announcement during the session, holding up the certificate as if to prove it was real. Nina's name had been listed among entries from schools with literary magazines and funded art departments. Molly was halfway through planning a small in-session celebration before the Resonance admin staff even caught wind of it.

But once they did, the machine kicked in. Vivienne forwarded the announcement to the entire board within an hour. By the next morning, Nina's story was featured on Resonance's web site alongside pull quotes about "nurturing hidden voices" and "creative empowerment."

At school the next day, the news had already made the rounds. Someone in the front office printed it and posted it on the bulletin board near the main stairs.

Madison overheard a teacher mention Nina by name in the hallway. She spoke of it in a muffled voice, as if unsure it was real—surprised, even, that someone like Nina had won. Not cruel. Just the kind of surprise reserved for people who were never expected to stand out.

At lunch, Nina was beaming. She brought the certificate, folded gently in her notebook as if it were something precious she wanted to keep close.

Abigail read it first. "You're a finalist?"

Nina nodded; eyes wide.

"That's amazing," Abigail said. And she meant it.

Lydia skimmed the paper. "I didn't know they did contests for this kind of thing." She smiled, but only slightly.

Madison said nothing at first. Just took the paper, looked it over, and handed it back. But then she smiled at Nina and said, "You should be proud. That's not nothing."

She watched Nina start to change—not in a bad way. Just... shift. She sat straighter. Talked more. Started brushing her hair differently, in a way that framed her face. She smiled easily. She belonged, now. Or at least, she looked like she did.

Later that week at breakfast, Vivienne was all business. She tapped her spoon twice against the rim of her teacup before saying to no one in particular, "This could be it."

Madison didn't look up from her toast. "What could?"

"The contest. Nina. The recognition. If we position it right, it could bring Resonance some real national visibility—and, more importantly, new donors who care about the arts. People love a success story."

She said it lightly, but Madison heard the calculation under it. The way Vivienne always did when something looked too perfect not to use.

"She's a good writer," Madison said.

Vivienne smiled. "Not just that. She's the right writer…
at the right time."

Madison didn't answer. But by that afternoon, the
branding had begun.

Nina's name had become a tagline. Vivienne began introducing Nina as "our rising star." The way people do
when they're collecting stories like stamps.

Madison said all the right things. She smiled at the photo
ops. Clapped when Nina read aloud at the next workshop showcase. But inside, Madison wondered how long
it would take before the light shifted.

Nina believed it was all about the story that she
wrote—the garden, the growth, the joy of imagination.
She didn't realize that the story wasn't hers anymore.

But Madison saw it. And she knew Nina didn't.

At least not yet.

CHAPTER TWENTY-TWO

The Missing

Nina didn't come to school on Monday.

Or Tuesday.

By Wednesday, Abigail asked if anyone had seen her. Lydia shrugged and said maybe she was sick. Madison didn't say anything. But she noticed—noticed the empty seat in homeroom, the untouched locker down the hall, the silence at lunch where Nina's small voice used to chime in just a beat late.

By Thursday, Madison checked the attendance sheet outside homeroom. Only one mark by Nina's name: "unexcused."

By Friday, someone else had set their tray down at the end of the bench without hesitation, like the space had never belonged to anyone else at all.

A weekend came and went, and by Monday, her name wasn't called in roll. That was when Madison felt it settle. This wasn't temporary.

She told herself it didn't matter. Girls left Ashmore all the time—new cities, new schools, family moves. But this felt... different. Too quiet. Too unfinished. Madison couldn't stop thinking about that cardigan Nina used to wear, the way she folded her papers like she was afraid of creasing them. You don't just vanish like that.

But she did.

No one really knew what had become of her.

There were rumors, of course. She'd just transferred. Or she'd gotten some writing scholarship to an arts school. One girl said she ran away with a musician. Another claimed she had entered witness protection. Madison heard all of them, but none of them sounded right.

The truth came quietly.

A week or so later, Molly pulled Madison aside after a workshop session at Resonance. The usual chime of her bracelets was missing. She looked tired; her smile thin.

"I just wanted you to know that I heard something about Nina," she said, carefully. "There was an incident..."

Madison blinked. "What kind of incident?"

Molly paused, her expression tightening with quiet concern. "Something happened at home. It was serious—police were involved."

Madison stepped in closer, her voice low. "Is she OK?"

Molly looked down for a moment, rubbing her hand along her arm. "I don't know," she breathed out. "I've tried to find out more, but no one's saying anything."

Madison waited for more details, but Molly didn't have any.

On her way out, Madison passed Vivienne in the Resonance hallway. She didn't plan to stop, but something in her paused.

"Did you ever hear what happened to Nina?" she asked.

Vivienne blinked. "Nina?"

"The girl from the writing workshop. Your *rising star*," Madison said.

There was a pause. "Oh," Vivienne said finally, too brightly. "That one. No, I haven't heard anything. Why?"

"No reason," Madison said, and walked on.

Back at school, no one seemed to know what to do with the space Nina had left behind. Her name still sat on the group project lists. A few of her books were left in her locker. Her handwriting lined the margins of a shared reading log. But the girl herself—gone.

Lydia had stopped bringing her up. Abigail mentioned her less and less. Eventually not at all.

By the following week, it was as though Nina had been a guest—someone who visited for a time and then left without saying goodbye.

Madison was flipping through a book at the Ashmore library when a counselor approached her. He was new. Kind eyes. Sweater vest. He said Madison's name with a soft voice, like he was trying to be gentle.

"I heard you were close with Nina."

Madison closed her notebook. "We worked together sometimes."

"Well, I just wanted to check in. See how you're doing. Something like this... it can be disorienting. Hard to process."

Madison nodded, not offering anything.

"It's okay to be sad that Nina's gone," he said. "She was your friend."

Madison looked at him, evenly.

"Not really."

That afternoon, she sat at the lunch table with Abigail and Lydia. The conversation picked up where it always did. Nothing out of place. Nothing left to explain.

It was back to being just the three of them.

Just like that.

CHAPTER TWENTY-THREE

The Concert for One

Aunt Mattie never announced her visits.

The knock wasn't on the front door so much as through the house itself. A brisk, unapologetic rhythm, followed by the unmistakable sweep of a voice: "Where's my niece? Don't tell me she's been practicing scales so endlessly she's forgotten that music is meant to move people, not just fingers."

Miss Hilliard's metronome froze mid-tick. Madison's fingers hovered above the piano keys. Silence pooled in the music room.

The door opened before anyone could object. Aunt Mattie swept in with a flare of patterned sleeves and a scarf far too bright for the somber room. Her presence filled the space the way the first bold note of a song breaks silence.

Even the portraits along the wall seemed to tilt askew, as if forced to acknowledge her arrival.

"Mrs. Renshaw," Miss Hilliard began, her voice taut with reprimand. "We're in the middle of—"

"Oh, poise and posture, I'm sure," Mattie interrupted, fluttering her fan. "Don't mind me. I adore a good scale. But I'd like to hear a real song—one of your pieces, darling. Play on." She perched herself in the corner chair as though she had been invited, crossing one leg over the other with theatrical leisure.

Madison hesitated, her hands still hovering. She looked to Miss Hilliard, who caught the glance. Miss Hilliard's jaw tightened by the barest of fractions. After a pause, Miss Hilliard inclined her head with reluctance, conceding the choice.

Madison reached forward and quietly changed the sheet on the stand, selecting a piece she thought Mattie might actually enjoy. Then she drew a breath and began. The melody unfurled gently, carrying a warmth that loosened the stillness.

Mattie leaned back, eyes half-closed, as if she were tasting the sound itself. A satisfied smile curled across her lips. "There she is," she murmured. "Not the little automaton, but my Maddie."

Madison's cheeks warmed, though her posture never slipped. Each phrase built into the next, until even the curtains seemed to stir with the sound. The space, usually rigid with rules, felt momentarily alive.

Miss Hilliard adjusted her papers noticeably, as if reassembling a boundary she'd just watched collapse. It was a small, pointed reclaiming of space. Mattie hadn't just interrupted the lesson; she had overturned the hierarchy of the afternoon.

The piece ended on a soft cadence. Madison let the final note linger, then lowered her hands to her lap, fingers folding neatly in practiced composure. For a moment, no one moved.

Then Mattie clapped lightly, more delighted than polite. "Lovely. That's what music is meant to be."

Miss Hilliard gathered her things with precision. "Tomorrow at the usual time," she said with clipped restraint. She excused herself with only the slightest glance at Mattie, a look that acknowledged Mattie's authority with disinclined deference.

Madison sat very still, pulse quickened by both the playing and the disruption. She wasn't used to having her practice commandeered. And yet, there had been something freeing in it.

Lucille appeared in the doorway as if on cue, holding a tea tray. "Mrs. Renshaw asked for this to be set in the sunroom, Duchess."

Madison blinked. "You knew she was coming?"

Mattie winked. "Someone in this house ought to be in on the plot. Now come along—let's have tea. A civilized rebellion against routine."

As Madison rose, she felt a tug of memory: her father standing in the doorway with a mint and a conspiratorial smile. That had been a rescue; this was a raid.

Both made her heart lift.

CHAPTER TWENTY-FOUR

The Tea

The sunroom was awash with late light.

The glass panes caught the afternoon glow, and the scent of roses drifted faintly in from the garden, threading with the cooler salt of the sea air. On the table waited Lucille's tray—China cups, sugared biscuits, and a teapot resting warm for them.

Mattie lowered herself into a chair with a rustle of scarves, making the room feel suddenly hers. She fanned herself once, then let the fan close with a snap. "Now this," she said, "is far preferable to drills and arpeggios."

Madison sat opposite, posture composed, though her pulse still carried the rhythm of what she'd played. She folded her hands on her lap; eyes fixed on her aunt.

Mattie tilted her head, studying her with a fondness that still carried an edge. "The piece you chose—there was something in it. You sounded like you had something to say, even if your teacher would rather you kept silent."

Madison lowered her gaze, the corner of her mouth shifting. "Well, Miss Hilliard—"

"Miss Hilliard. Doesn't like being reminded she isn't the star of the room," Mattie cut in, arching a brow. "But you, my Maddie—you've a gift in those hands. Something no posture drill will ever teach."

The nickname landed with its usual weight. Maddie. So near to Mattie's own name it felt claimed, as though her aunt had pressed a seal upon her. Madison let the thought settle, equal parts comfort and tether.

Mattie poured the tea with a hand too careless for ceremony. "You wouldn't believe it, but your grandfather loved music once. When your grandmother was alive, he danced with her and even dabbled at the piano."

Madison blinked. "Grandfather plays piano?"

"Badly," Mattie said with a dry smile. "But with feeling. At least he used to. He was very different before your grandmother passed. He laughed then. He wasn't always carved from stone."

Madison stirred her cup slowly. The thought of Alastair laughing and playing the piano felt foreign, like recalling a story from another family altogether.

Mattie caught her expression and softened. "Difficult to fathom, isn't it? But it's true. Before grief hardened him, he was witty, even playful—much like your father." Mattie's voice wavered against her will, and she looked away. Toward the window where the light was beginning to fade.

Madison felt her chest tighten.

Mattie composed herself with a sigh, her gaze returning to Madison. "I think about your father often, especially lately. Without him here, I know it's harder for you."

Madison uncharacteristically opened up before she could stop herself. "It had been getting easier, actually, but that article dragged me backward. The one in Newport Monthly. They wrote as if they knew him. For a moment it made me wonder how much I actually did."

Mattie's fan snapped open with defiance. "Rubbish. They don't know him—not as you did. No article can steal that. What was between you and your father belongs to you. Don't ever let ink on a page convince you otherwise."

Madison let out a breath she hadn't realized she held. The sting lingered but dulled beneath her aunt's certainty.

Mattie's hand lingered on the handle of her cup. "I remember losing my own father. I was older than you, but it hurt all the same. He was special to me—the way your father was to you."

Madison smiled faintly, seeing her aunt relatable in a kinship she hadn't expected. "I wish I could have known him."

"He would have loved you, Maddie," Mattie said softly. "You remind me of him sometimes—sharp eyes, quiet in a room but never unseeing. He was the one who taught me to keep true in a family so given to pretense."

Mattie's eyes grew distant, softened by memory. For a moment she seemed far away. Then she blinked, her expression shifting from soft reminiscence to something more pointed. "But dwelling on the past won't prepare you for what's coming."

She reached for a biscuit, broke it with deliberate precision. "Alastair isn't getting any younger. He's well past the age most people retire, yet he refuses to step aside. He's watching. Measuring."

Madison tilted her head. "Measuring what?"

Mattie's eyes narrowed. "Who might fill the void your father left."

The words hit harder than Madison expected, heavy as stones in her chest. Her cup wavered, and she set it down with care, giving a soft chime against the saucer.

"Beatrix is in Paris," Mattie went on and scoffed, "playing foreign politics like she's a countess. Ned? Timid as a rabbit, no head for business. The rest are gone. There's no one left in that generation who can do it."

"So, what's he going to do?" Madison asked, uncertain.

She leaned forward, tone shifting. "The search must fall lower. To your generation. Alastair is old-fashioned. He sees a male successor. That's why he clings to August, and Clarisse fans it like a flame. But August is soft. He'll be eaten alive."

She let that settle a moment, then added, quieter, "So that's where you come in. Whether you asked for it or not, his gaze will eventually fall to you."

Madison said nothing. She felt it already—every time she saw him, the weight of his eyes, the silent judgment that came with it, like standing on a scale that never tipped.

Mattie's fingers tapped once against the porcelain like punctuation. "If you want to survive this circus, you'll need more than just politeness and poise. You'll have to use your wits. Those sharp eyes of yours—see what they'd rather you didn't. Read the room while others are too focused on themselves."

Madison held her gaze and nodded slowly. The words felt more like a dare than advice.

Mattie's voice softened for the last time. "You're becoming a young woman, Maddie. Just don't let your mother polish you so much until all that's left is her own reflection. Be more. "

"Be you."

CHAPTER TWENTY-FIVE

The Curtain Rises

Soft bulbs hummed on the antique mirror.

Lucille's hands moved with slow precision, fastening the final pearl at the nape of Madison's neck. The girl sat still, spine straight, dress pristine—a slip of white silk that fell like poured milk over her frame. Not bridal, not childish. But intentional. It whispered of innocence, but the cut signaled her maturity.

"You'll stop hearts tonight, Duchess," Lucille murmured. "Just don't let yours be one of them."

Madison didn't smile. She merely looked at her reflection, head slightly tilted, studying it the way one might study an opponent—coolly, distantly, with a kind of unspoken negotiation passing between the girl she was and the woman she was expected to be.

There was a quiet knock before the door eased open, and Vivienne stepped into the room. She didn't speak right away, only looked at Madison in the mirror—her eyes scanning, calculating, approving. Then, without a word, she crossed the room and adjusted one of the pearls Lucille had already fastened.

"There," Vivienne said softly, her voice more present than performative. "Perfect."

It wasn't affection, exactly. But it was something. An acknowledgment. Madison gave a slight nod, and that was the end of it. They understood each other better now—not tenderly, but with clarity.

Madison was fifteen going on sixteen, but tonight she would be more. Her mother had curated Madison's debut into society—not a true debutante ball, but something adjacent. A charity gala for Resonance. A night for patrons, artists, and legacy families. But Madison knew what it really was.

A performance.

The venue, an old Newport estate turned gallery, glowed under string lights and glass. Guests arrived in waves: donors in tailored tuxedos, women wrapped in chiffon, teenage girls on the edge of womanhood, boys posturing in too-large jackets. The scent of champagne hung in the air.

Vivienne floated from guest to guest, wine glass always half full, voice feather-soft with just enough volume to command a circle. She greeted them all by name, touching elbows lightly, nodding at whispered compliments. Her speech, when it finally came, was brief and lovely:

"Tonight, we celebrate not just art, but the future—the hands that will shape it. Our daughters, our sons. May they find beauty, and may they carry it forward."

The applause was polite. Practiced.

Madison moved through the crowd with quiet ease. Every nod, every glance, every smile landed exactly where she placed it. She accepted compliments with practiced grace. Older women cooed at her composure; younger boys tripped over their words. She acknowledged and thanked, always moving, never lingering.

She spotted Lydia first—surrounded by a group of older boys, laughing at jokes not meant for her. Her gown was a little too tight, her hair overly styled, but it worked. Lydia always knew how to hold attention, even if it was borrowed.

Abigail hovered nearby, arms crossed, eyes scanning the paintings rather than the people. She looked unimpressed by the decor, the guest list, the entire premise. When Madison brushed past, Abigail leaned in just enough to mutter, "They should've used the money on new instruments instead of this absurd chandelier."

Madison didn't disagree. But she only smiled in return, the way she always did when Abigail was right but missing the point.

Then she turned back to the flow of guests, the practiced rhythm of mingling pressing her onward.

Near the gallery's back wall, she passed a small cluster of older men in quiet conversation. One of them looked up and offered a gentle smile—Mattie's husband, Harrison Renshaw. He was rarely alone in public, almost always with Mattie at his side.

"Uncle Harrison," Madison greeted politely.

"Madison," he said, offering a slight bow of his head. "You're a vision tonight. Your aunt will take full credit, of course."

"Is she here?" Madison replied, glancing around.

He chuckled, dry and light. "You think I would be here if she hadn't dragged me?"

Madison smirked faintly.

"Enjoy yourself," he added. "Just not too much. The old guard's watching."

Madison grinned and nodded, "Let them."

Madison made her way toward the drink alcove, where a small circle parted to let her through. There stood Aunt Mattie—champagne in one hand, the other resting lightly on the edge of the counter as if the whole evening bored her stiff.

"Well," Mattie drawled, her gaze skimming Madison, then the room. "They've dressed the prize lamb well enough for auction. It's a shame most of the bidders are blind and the rest as dim as candle stubs."

Madison arched a brow. "Good thing I'm not for sale."

Mattie chuckled, low and warm. "No, you're not. You're watching the auctioneer, and that's far more dangerous."

Madison shifted her gaze toward the room. "And who is the auctioneer tonight?"

Mattie gave a knowing look. "Depends on who you ask. Half the room thinks they are—including your mother. But the real auctioneer?"

She took a slow sip of champagne. "Hasn't arrived yet."

Mattie leaned in and took Madison by the hands, her tone softening just a shade in admiration. "You carry the room better than your mother ever did. There's steel under that silk—quiet, polished, and not meant to bend."

Madison inclined her head—not in gratitude, but recognition.

Mattie grinned. "Good girl. Now go smile at someone important and confuse them."

And with that, Madison stepped back into the current, the air around her tinged now with a sharper edge.

The next scene was waiting.

And Madison knew her lines by heart.

CHAPTER TWENTY-SIX

The Auctioneer

They felt his presence before they saw him.

A hush moved through the room—not silence, exactly, but restraint. Conversations quieted, postures straightened, laughter was clipped short. Alastair La Croix had arrived.

He entered without announcement, without entourage. Just authority.

He stood near the rear of the hall, one hand behind his back, his expression unreadable. He moved alone, unhurried, surveying the room like a man long used to walking into his own narrative. His gaze moved through the crowd like a surveyor marking fault lines—quiet, exacting, inevitable.

Madison felt it immediately—the subtle rebalancing. The weight of expectations shifting corners. Even Vivienne, who had been gliding through the evening like a practiced hostess, faltered just slightly. Her smile held, but her shoulders tightened, and her laugh no longer reached her eyes.

The auctioneer was here.

Madison looked toward him and caught his eyes in her direction. For once, the weight of his gaze didn't pass over her. It held. And for the first time, she didn't feel invisible. She felt seen. Even considered.

One of the Resonance board members hovered near, clearly waiting to be acknowledged. When Madison turned slightly toward him, he seized the moment. "Your grandfather makes quite the entrance," he said, his voice trying for casual but landing somewhere closer to reverent.

"Better than mine?" Madison asked, her tone airy, but her smile just a shade too knowing to be sweet.

He blinked, as if thrown off by the reply. By the time he regrouped, she had already turned away.

Her attention was interrupted by a second entrance—less commanding but designed to be noticed.

August Wexley strolled in well after her grandfather, every step deliberate, every gesture practiced. His grin was handsome, his posture exact, poised on the surface. But there was a glint of self-satisfaction in the way he smoothed his lapel, collecting glances as though they confirmed what he believed.

He made his way through a knot of teenage girls and gave a practiced nod to one of the photographers stationed near the floral arch. Then he approached Madison.

"Cousin," he said with a smirk, drawing out the word like a title. "You look... appropriately radiant."

Madison turned, expression composed. "And you're late."

He shrugged, adjusting a cuff. "Had to keep the suspense alive."

As the two of them spoke, Madison noticed some of the older women whispering to each other, eyes in their direction.

August had always carried whispers with him. Raised by his grandmother Clarisse—Alastair's eldest sister, known for her iron will—he was the polished remnant of a family scandal. His mother, Vivica, had died young in a fire that no one ever mentioned. Clarisse stepped in, and over the years, she shaped and spoiled him in equal measure.

For all his preening, August was the only male in the family coming of age—an accident of birth that lent his antics more consequence than they deserved. In certain circles, he was spoken of as Alastair's heir apparent, though the mantle sat poorly on him.

August stared past her shoulder, eyes tracking a group of girls near the refreshment table. He was watching them all the same way, like they were items in a gallery curated for his pleasure—every smile, every sparkle, every strap of silk.

"You should try blinking," Madison offered. "It makes the exhibits feel less self-conscious."

August didn't flinch. "Just appreciating the installation. Some of the work is derivative, but the framing's exquisite."

He brushed past her toward the girls, and quipped, "but looks can be deceiving. I should probably inspect the art up close."

Then he glanced over his shoulder at Madison and said, "Some pieces are a bit too curated to take seriously."

Then he pivoted back toward the girls, satisfied with his parting shot.

Before she could reply, another presence slipped in—quieter, more controlled than August. Vivienne. Her hand grazed Madison's arm in a gesture so casual it was practically staged.

"Madison, darling," she said with her signature coo. "I hope he's not boring you. The last thing we need tonight is an unflattering quote in the press."

Vivienne's smile didn't waver, but her eyes flicked—first to August, then to the watching crowd, calculating exposure in real time.

Madison let out a breath through her nose. "He's exhausting," she muttered. "Like a mirror that won't stop talking."

Vivienne's grip on Madison's arm firmed, a silent directive cloaked in poise. Then, as if to soften the command, she smoothed a hand along Madison's shoulder and leaned in just slightly.

"I spoke with Clarisse earlier," she said, her voice honeyed but firm. "She thought it fitting for the two of you to open the evening with the first dance. Symbolic, naturally—not sentimental. I'm sure you understand."

Before Madison could respond, Vivienne moved closer. "She's been coughing more lately," Vivienne added, just loud enough for Madison to hear. "It's important that the family appears aligned tonight. I trust you'll do what's necessary."

Vivienne's smile didn't falter, but her hand lingered a bit too long on Madison's shoulder.

Madison understood. A dance wasn't much. Just for show, like Vivienne said.

But in this family, shows mattered. Especially to someone like Alastair, who treated every small gesture like a test. And tonight, Madison didn't just plan to pass—she meant to redefine the curve.

Across the room, Mattie had joined Alastair. Madison saw the way he winced at something she said, the slight flash of irritation behind his eyes. Whatever Mattie had offered him—a barb, a truth, a joke—had landed. He recovered quickly, of course, but the crease at the corner of his mouth lingered longer than it should have.

Near the stage, the musicians began to take their places, tuning strings, shuffling sheet music. The entire room seemed to adjust with them. Not loudly, but undeniably. A held breath before the first note of a song, a hush born from anticipation.

The room was ready, though none of them knew for what.

CHAPTER TWENTY-SEVEN

The Waltz

The quiet was spreading.

Madison stood near the edge of the room, composed but alert, watching as the floor slowly began to clear. This was the moment. The first formal dance of the night. A shift in tempo, a shift in power. Partners would be chosen, expectations confirmed, eyes drawn.

August stood beside her, his posture casual, his attention anything but.

"August," she said, voice warm and smooth, "I think you'll enjoy meeting someone."

He blinked, then grinned—more to himself than to her—and fell into step like it had been his idea all along.

Madison led him to the side of the room with quiet grace. They passed clusters of murmuring guests until she spotted Lydia—standing near the perimeter, laughing at something Abigail had clearly dismissed. Her dress caught the light just enough, her posture inviting and unguarded.

"Lydia," Madison said, placing a gentle hand on her arm. "May I introduce August Wexley, my cousin."

August bowed, just enough to suggest manners without sincerity. "Charmed," he said, gaze dragging over her in a slow, appraising sweep.

Lydia's reaction was instant—eyes bright, a breath caught halfway between surprise and delight. She turned to Madison with a glint of mischief—half-flattered, half-calculating. "Now this," Lydia said under her breath, "is the kind of cousin you should've introduced sooner."

August gave a quick laugh, flattered but dismissive. "Funny how that works," he muttered, voice low, eyes glancing to Madison. He started to pivot away, clearly reading the orchestration—but the corner of his mouth twitched, betraying an interest he hadn't yet decided to indulge.

Lydia stepped into his view before he could finish the turn. Her smile was deliberate now—a dare, not a plea. "I didn't realize you were shy," she said lightly. She lifted her chin, subtly drawing herself taller, her shoulders angling back just enough to suggest a practiced awareness of posture—and the effect it had.

That stopped him. His brows lifted, the derision slipping into something almost entertained. He let out a quieter scoff, "Hardly."

Madison watched the spark between them—quick, potent, the kind that burned fast and loud. "You two should dance," she said, breezy and benevolent.

Lydia glanced once more at Madison, then smoothed the fabric at her hip and took August by the arm. By the time Madison turned away, they were already moving toward the floor, gravity doing the rest.

Madison moved quickly through the crowd with quiet purpose. Past the columns, near the musicians, she found him—Julian Reeves. They had danced before. Back when lessons were more obligation than art. He had always been quiet, careful, precise. Never too eager. Never sloppy. He stood now with his hands clasped behind his back, watching the room rather than anyone in it, the kind of restraint she could trust.

She offered her hand. "Shall we?"

He took it with a small, steady nod—something flickering behind his eyes. Flattered, perhaps. Curious, maybe. But also surprised, as if he'd expected her to choose someone older, more prominent, someone whose name mattered. But he said nothing, only met her gaze with quiet resolve. He didn't ask why she chose him. And that, too, made him the right choice.

They stepped toward the dance floor just as the music began, timing folding around them like an invitation only they had been given. Madison didn't lead—not in name—but every pivot, every glide echoed her intent. She could feel the eyes on her—measuring, admiring, comparing. She gave them nothing but precision.

Julian followed seamlessly—almost. There was a half-beat, early on, where he hesitated, his foot catching just short of hers. Not a stumble, not quite—but an instant of uncertainty that passed through his grip before he adjusted. Madison didn't flinch. She let the moment smooth itself out and moved forward as if she hadn't noticed, which of course meant everyone else wouldn't either. He recovered quickly, falling into step, giving her the room to command without ever making it look like she was in control.

Vivienne appeared at the edge of the crowd. Her smile was taut, her expression composed but betrayed by a pinch of tightness around the eyes. She hovered there, gaze flicking first to August and Lydia—then to Madison.

Madison didn't need to hear a word to know what Vivienne was thinking. The tension in her posture said enough. She was angry. And worried. Angry that Madison had broken from the plan. Worried that the narrative had changed, and that she hadn't written it.

Around them, dancers spun and stumbled. Abigail kept perfect time with her partner, mouthing the counts of the one-two-three tempo. August twirled Lydia with too much flourish, throwing her slightly off balance. She giggled, recovering quickly, but his hand went to her waist too long, and they missed the next step entirely.

Madison remained steady, centered in a way that made the chaos around her feel incidental.

Their movements circled outward, measured and luminous. Each turn brought her closer to the heart of the room, where chandeliers gathered the light like crowns above a court. And when the final note hung in the air, she stopped precisely in the center—head lifted, back straight, calm and composed.

For a second, no one moved. Madison exhaled slowly, just once, and then clapping followed like a cue. Then applause rippled through the space—polite at first, then swelling as if the entire room had collectively realized who they were clapping for. Not the dance. Not the music. Her.

Vivienne watched from across the room. She joined the applause, her smile practiced, eyes never leaving Madison. It was a proud smile, yes—but also opportunistic. She knew how to claim a share of someone else's spotlight without saying a word.

But no one looked at her.

Madison didn't turn or curtsy. She didn't need to. The applause wasn't a surprise—it was confirmation. She let it wash over her like stage light, standing still, unmoved, letting the moment settle where it belonged.

Her eyes found Alastair's across the crowd. He did not smile. He did not applaud. But he tilted his head ever so slightly. Not warmth. Not pride. But recognition.

Mattie leaned in beside him, eyes locked on Madison.

"That one... is a La Croix."

CHAPTER TWENTY-EIGHT

The Ask

The banner drooped across the hallway, heavy with expectation.

The courtyard was alive with rumors and awkward teenage negotiations. Flyers fluttered. Girls paced in groups like swans rehearsing entrances, flinching every time they passed a boy. The boys, in turn, looked perpetually startled—like animals aware of the trap, but too afraid not to step into it. Homecoming had been announced at Ashmore.

It was their sophomore year. Madison, Lydia, and Abigail were no longer the wide-eyed newcomers—they had been replaced by a fresh crop of awkward boys and girls still bumping into walls and mispronouncing teacher names. The trio had settled into their rhythms: Madison the quiet center, Lydia the orbiting spark, Abigail the unshakable satellite.

The three of them sat at one of the outdoor lunch tables, trays partially eaten, sun dappled through the branches overhead. Lydia kept tugging at the ends of her sleeves, her eyes sharp with anticipation. "I swear, if someone doesn't ask me soon, I'm going to lose my mind."

"It's a manufactured anxiety spiral," Abigail muttered, stabbing her fruit cup. "Pair people off, pump them full of sugar and hormones, then watch them combust. It's like a social experiment designed by sadists."

Madison just smiled and took a sip of her water, eyes half-lidded. She didn't say a word. But she was watching—carefully. The way boys passed their table with clumsy bravado, how some glanced too long and others didn't look at all. She read the signs like a language only she remembered how to speak.

It suddenly got quiet as a shadow fell across their table.

It was Noah Thorne—senior, lacrosse captain, model jawline. He had a reputation for confidence that never quite tipped into arrogance, and a talent for making everyone feel like they'd just been chosen. He wasn't supposed to talk to underclassmen unless they were injured—or spectacular. He was holding a folded note in one hand—the kind meant to be private but timed for an audience.

"Madison," he said, smiling like it was obvious. "You going to Homecoming?"

Abigail froze mid-bite. Lydia stopped breathing.

Madison looked up. Blinked once.

"Maybe."

Noah waited.

Madison shifted in her seat, plucked an invisible thread from her sleeve, and sighed. It wasn't cruel, not even dismissive. It was bored.

And that—more than any sharp word—was enough. The confidence that had carried him over to the table peeled back.

"Guess I'll go somewhere less terrifying."

He walked away trying to look unshaken.

After he got to a safe distance, heads turned. Lydia shrieked, "Are you insane?"

"He's not..." Madison trailed off, like the word hadn't earned her time.

"Noah Thorne just asked you to Homecoming!"

"Technically, he *didn't* ask me."

"But he's, like, *the* guy. He's literally perfect."

Madison smirked slightly and looked Lydia in the eye: "Then why don't you go with him?"

Lydia blinked in stunned disbelief.

"I mean it," Madison said seriously. "He'd be lucky."

Lydia flushed. "Really? But he'd never..." Her voice faded.

Abigail, quiet until now, finally said, "You really don't like him, do you?"

"No," Madison said. "But he likes attention. And Lydia's got that in spades."

She stood, smoothing her skirt. Then, without another word, she turned and walked across the courtyard toward the senior table.

Conversation died instantly. The boys there straightened, stammered, a few of them blinking like deer in headlights. None of them met her eyes.

Noah leaned back, trying to look amused. "Change your mind?"

Madison gave a calm, confident breath. "No."

She let that sit for a moment, then glanced back over her shoulder—toward Lydia, who was still watching in fearful awe.

"Lydia doesn't have a date yet," Madison said smoothly, her voice just loud enough for the others to hear.

Noah hesitated. "I was kind of hoping to go with you."

Madison tilted her head, lips curved just slightly. "You should ask her. I'd owe you."

That hung in the air like light perfume—vague but lingering.

Noah stared at her for a second too long. The smirk faded. He shifted, caught between pride and surrender. His hand was still clenched around the note.

Madison gave him the faintest shrug. "So, what are you waiting for?"

That did it.

Noah stood, straightened his jacket, and walked toward the sophomore tables. Every step seemed to echo. Lydia's eyes went wide as he approached, and when he finally stopped in front of her and muttered something, she didn't answer at first. Then nodded. Hard. Like if she didn't, she might miss her only chance.

From the senior boys' table, Madison watched the whole thing. The other boys at the table sat frozen in silence, none of them daring to speak—let alone make eye contact.

She rose, unhurried, and walked back across the courtyard. As she passed Noah, she gave him a look—enough to scramble whatever resolve he still had.

When she reached the girls' table again, Lydia exploded in a squeal that turned every nearby head. Abigail didn't squeal. She just looked at Madison — not smiling, not blinking — as if she'd just watched something beautiful burn and couldn't decide whether to mourn it or applaud.

Madison sat down slowly, graceful as ever, and reached for her water like nothing had happened at all.

It was almost too easy.

CHAPTER TWENTY-NINE

The Assembly

Lydia had retouched her mascara three times before second period and kept checking the exits like she was afraid Noah might bolt and revoke his offer. Her voice pitched between dreamy sighs and absolute dread.

"I just can't believe it. I mean, I know you set it up, but still — it's Noah Thorne," she whispered as they walked in.

"Believe it," Madison said without looking up.

Abigail was focused on something else entirely. "His name is Dr. Ivo Merrick. He's not really psychic — it's just cold reading and nonverbal suggestion. People don't realize how much they give away by simply standing still."

Lydia blinked at her. "Do you think he can tell me who I'm going to marry? What if he says Noah?"

"You'll probably tell him first," Abigail muttered.

Madison said nothing. She was scanning the auditorium. The room was already full — juniors and seniors up front, first-year students wedged in the back. Teachers lined the walls like sentries.

They called it an "Enrichment Experience," which was Ashmore's way of justifying an expensive excuse to interrupt class. The entire school had been herded into the auditorium for a special mid-week assembly.

Dr. Merrick stepped onto the stage precisely on time. He wore a soft charcoal suit and had that cultivated stillness that made everyone else fidget. A portable whiteboard stood beside him. No assistants. No props. Just a marker in one hand and a subtle smile.

He launched right in. No introduction. No flourish.

"You," he pointed at someone in the front row. "Stand up."

"What's your favorite color?"

The student looked around, embarrassed and uncertain.

"You seem like a pretty cool guy. I'm guessing..." He turned, wrote something on the board, then looked back.

"Ok, what is it?"

"I guess... blue?" the student stammered.

Dr. Merrick flipped the board around. It read: *"I guess... blue?"*

Laughter, then applause.

He moved quickly through the crowd, asking questions — easy ones at first: birth month, favorite food. Then harder: favorite band, childhood pet, first crush. Each time, he got it right.

The auditorium erupted. Again, and again.

Madison watched. Not the show — the method. He was excellent, but not magic. His questions narrowed the field. "Is it a short name?" "Low or high?" "Let's go through the alphabet—a, b, c..."

It wasn't foolproof. But it was enough.

Abigail leaned over and whispered, "See? It's just reading people. Not minds."

After several routines, Dr. Merrick paused and scanned the crowd. "One final volunteer. Someone special."

Hands shot up. Lydia's was the highest. She looked like she might levitate.

He looked toward her row, then past her. Then back again.

"You," he said, pointing at Madison. "Auburn hair. Come on up."

Madison stood, smiled, and walked with effortless poise to the stage. The room settled— boys leaning forward, girls glancing around. The kind of silence that pressed in from all sides.

Dr. Merrick faced the audience, then turned back to her.

"I think I already know the question everyone wants answered," he said with a grin. "With Homecoming coming up, they all want to know: Who would *you* like to go with?"

A wave of whispers swept through the auditorium. Then silence — taut and waiting.

Madison didn't flinch. She smiled. Elegant. Composed. Then raised one eyebrow like it was a secret not worth sharing.

Dr. Merrick studied her. His expression shifted — not confusion, not awe. Just... uncertainty.

"I've never had this happen before," he said softly, feigning both concern and dejection. "Nothing. I've got no idea."

The audience stirred. Madison's smile held steady.

He let the silence stretch. Then grinned like he'd cracked the final number in an unsolvable code. "Never mind. There it is."

He picked up the marker again, now more animated. He tried phrases:

"They're in this room, aren't they?" "You've already made up your mind." "Does it start with an A?"

Each time, Madison gave him nothing. Not a glance. Not a shrug. Not a blink too slow.

"You're a tough one," he quipped quietly with a smirk.

"But I've got it." He turned slightly, shielding the board, and wrote something quickly.

"All right, tell them who," he said.

The auditorium leaned forward in anticipation.

Madison's eyes narrowed and smile widened. She shook her head no.

Dr. Merrick stepped beside her and showed the board — only to her.

Her expression didn't change, but her eyes flickered with something like recognition. Or even concern.

"It's okay," he said gently. "I'm not going to reveal it."

He stepped back. "Am I right?"

She nodded slowly, conceding he was correct.

He erased the board in a single, clean stroke without showing it.

"Give it up for Madison," he said.

The auditorium erupted in applause and cheers.

Madison walked back down the steps and returned to her seat between Lydia and Abigail. Neither of them said a word at first.

Then, as the crowd began to file out, Lydia grabbed her arm. "What did he write? Was it Noah? Tell me you didn't change your mind!"

"It wasn't Noah," Madison said reassuringly.

Abigail leaned in. "Come on, we saw your face. He got it right. You have to tell us. What did he write?"

Madison glanced between them, calm as ever.

They waited.

She gave them a small smile, but it wasn't playful or smug. It was final.

"Nobody."

CHAPTER THIRTY

The Leaving

The gym had been transformed.

String lights draped from the ceiling like vines. Tables lined the edges, candles flickering in glass votives. A small band played near the stage — upright bass, brushed drums, the mellow warmth of a saxophone. Not loud, not flashy. Just tasteful.

Neither of them had dates.

Nobody asked Abigail. Madison turned everyone down.

So, they went together — not in protest, not as a statement. Just... because it made sense.

Abigail wore navy blue, understated and clean. Madison chose something softer than what she had worn at the gala — a pale green silk that caught the light without begging for it. No sequins. No sparkle. Just elegance. She didn't need anything louder.

When they arrived, people turned. Not all at once — but enough.

Lydia was already there, surrounded. Her dress was louder than Madison's, shinier, tighter. Noah hovered behind her like a date without instructions. The energy around him hummed — surrounded by a loose ring of lacrosse teammates and their dates, cutting up loudly near the back. He laughed when they laughed, clapped shoulders, played along.

But when he looked toward Madison — and he did — it wasn't direct. More like his eyes brushed past her before he deliberately found something else to focus on.

The evening stretched on with a kind of suspended charm — soft music, shifting light, pockets of laughter that rose and fell like waves. Abigail kept pointing out things that annoyed her: the way the punch was too sweet, the couple slow dancing out of rhythm in the middle of the floor, the one girl in glitter boots who clearly hadn't read the dress code.

Madison listened, half-amused. Abigail's observations were sharp but not really mean. Just honest. And a little bit nervous. It was easier to focus on surface-level flaws than think about the people who hadn't asked her to come.

During a lull in the music, Madison stepped out into the hallway to cool off. That's when Noah approached.

Alone.

"You always look like you're watching something no one else can see," he said. His voice was quieter than usual. Slurred at the edges.

Madison didn't respond. Her posture shifted slightly — alert, guarded. She heard the thickness in his voice and didn't like the weight behind it.

Noah leaned against the wall beside her, not quite looking at her. "I guess nobody here was good enough for you," he said — like he meant it as a joke, but mostly just sounded like he was feeling sorry for himself.

Madison glanced at him. "It appears that way," she said, inching toward the door.

Noah looked down, then back at her. "What would it take for someone like me to ever matter to you?"

Madison didn't hesitate. "Nothing you can change."

Noah said nothing. His jaw tightened, and for a second, he looked like he might say more — but whatever it was collapsed inside him. He turned and walked back towards the auditorium. He paused at the door, just for a second. Then he disappeared back into the noise.

Madison watched the door. She wasn't sure if it was pity she felt, or relief.

She followed a few minutes later and saw Lydia by the punch table. Noah had returned to the circle of seniors, where a few boys were clearly passing something between plastic cups — not even trying to be subtle. The chaperones either hadn't noticed or were choosing not to.

Madison made her way over to Lydia, who was still glowing from the attention and the soft rhythm of the evening. "Enjoying yourself?" she asked, the words light but the look behind them careful.

Lydia beamed. "I really am. I didn't think it'd be like this. I mean, I knew it could be fun, but this feels like… I don't know. The real thing."

Madison nodded. She didn't say it, but she was glad that in this moment Lydia felt seen. She looked happy. Not grounded, not steady. Simply happy enough to follow the next good feeling out the door.

Not long after, Lydia drifted back toward the boys — back to the noise and attention, back to Noah.

Abigail came up beside Madison, watching Lydia walk off. "That girl's going to rewrite this night in her head a hundred different ways," she said. "Only one of them will be true."

Madison shrugged, quiet. "They'd all be true to her."

Soon after, Madison saw Noah lean into Lydia, saying something low. Lydia immediately turned to look at Madison. For a moment, her expression wavered — uncertainty, apology — and then it was gone. She turned and slowly followed him toward the door.

Lydia moved hesitantly — until Madison stepped in front of her.

"Don't," Madison said.

Lydia hesitated. "He just wants to get away from everything. Just for a while."

Madison didn't speak right away. She merely looked at Lydia — steady, clear, the kind of look that meant more than words.

Lydia bit her lip. "We're just going to go somewhere quiet. Just the two of us. Just for a bit."

Madison didn't move. "He's not going out there for quiet."

That landed, but not quite enough. Lydia gave her a look — part defiance, part pleading — and walked off into the night.

Madison stood there a moment longer. She didn't try to follow. She'd already said everything she was willing to say. She turned and walked back to Abigail.

She didn't say anything when she rejoined Abigail, but her expression said enough.

Abigail glanced toward the door. "Let me guess. They left."

Madison nodded once.

"Should we tell someone?" Abigail asked.

Madison's mouth tightened. "They'll figure it out."

It wasn't callous. But it wasn't warm, either.

Just the truth.

CHAPTER THIRTY-ONE

The Consequence

The phone rang late — muffled through layers of walls and carpet, but still enough to pull Madison from sleep. She sat up slowly, already knowing that it wasn't good. Calls at that hour never were.

Footsteps. A hallway light flicked on. Then a knock.

Lucille cracked open the door, silhouetted in the light.

"Duchess," she said softly. "There's been an accident."

Her voice was calm, but it wasn't steady.

Madison blinked. The words didn't land right away. They hovered in the air for a second — long enough to reach some older part of her memory.

Her father.

Lucille's voice fended something off — fear. That was the sound she remembered. Not the words. Just the break. The silence that followed.

"It's Lydia," Lucille said again, her voice pushing gently through Madison's daze.

Madison exhaled — slow, quiet, as if trying not to wake herself fully. The real world often holds terrors larger than any nightmare.

"She's bruised, but okay. The boy she was with... he was taken to the hospital."

Madison was awake now.

On Monday at school, the story had already splintered. The rumors multiplied fast, each one more embellished than the last — wilder, louder, harder to trace.

Some said he'd swerved to avoid an animal. Others said he was speeding to make curfew. One version insisted Lydia had been driving, which made absolutely no sense. There was talk of other people in the car, a second vehicle, even a lover's quarrel before they left. But none of it mattered. The truth — the quiet, sad version — had already settled.

They sat at lunch in near silence. Abigail picked at her sandwich. Madison stirred her soup but didn't eat. Lydia sat across from them, eyes glassy, her tray untouched.

It was true that Noah had been drinking.

After they left the dance, he took her to a quiet overlook — one of those out-of-the-way places people went when they didn't want to be found. Lydia had tried to lighten the mood, maybe even make it romantic, but Noah was somewhere else entirely. Brooding. Distant. Feeling sorry for himself in a way that didn't leave room for anyone else.

They talked for a while. Or she talked. He mostly stared at the dashboard. Eventually, he said he'd take her home.

That's when he hit the tree. He wasn't critically injured — a mild concussion and a broken ankle where his foot had braced too hard on the brake. It wasn't life-threatening, but it was enough. He was out for the season. Suspended from the lacrosse team. Possibly from school entirely — no one was sure yet.

Lydia got a deep bruise on her shoulder from the seatbelt — a sharp, purplish line that would take days to fade. She also got a reprimand in her file. Nothing serious. Just enough to leave a second mark — one on paper, one on skin.

She had also cried — a lot. But now she was quiet, red-eyed and shaking. She looked more angry than sad. Like she couldn't figure out who she was more upset at — him, or herself.

"I was so stupid," she whispered, her voice thin and cracking. "I knew better, and I still went."

Abigail reached across the table and lightly touched Lydia's hand. "That doesn't make you stupid," she said. "It makes you human."

Madison watched her carefully, quietly. Something pulled at her — a pressure behind the ribs, tight and dull. She would never say it aloud.

At another table, a girl was retelling the story like she'd been there — adding drama, subtracting truth. Across the courtyard, at Noah's usual table, a group of boys had gathered without him, but their glances kept drifting toward Lydia. One of them nudged another and whispered something.

Madison saw the way Lydia shrank slightly in her seat, her spine folding in on itself, for once not liking the attention. It was easy to forget how fast stories turned into weapons.

But Madison had set all of it in motion. She'd turned Noah away, left him suspended in that uneasy space between dismissal and unraveling. Whatever happened to him — maybe he brought it on himself.

But Lydia hadn't.

CHAPTER THIRTY-TWO

The Trip

The plane banked gently over the Seine.

Its engines hummed a lullaby as the city of Paris unfolded beneath them. Madison leaned toward the window, watching the river catch the light like a ribbon of glass. She didn't say anything, but beside her, Vivienne was smiling. Genuinely smiling. It was strange to see.

"This is a really big deal for Trixie," she said, glancing over. "She's receiving the key to the city. Can you believe that? The mayor himself is presenting it—something about her work in diplomacy and cultural preservation. It's a huge honor."

Madison gave a slow blink. Beatrix. In her mind, her aunt was still Beatrix: the elegant, distant sister of her late father, rarely mentioned and almost never seen. Trixie was Vivienne's word—casual and affectionate.

"I didn't know cities had keys," Madison murmured.

Vivienne gave a soft laugh. "It's symbolic. A thank-you from the city for everything she's done."

It was hard to picture. Madison had never thought of her aunt as someone who did anything. She existed in snapshots: poised in tailored dresses, attending funerals and weddings, always with a glass of wine and a slightly bored smile. But apparently, here in Paris, she was something else.

When they landed, Madison already knew the routine. Her uncle Charles—Ambassador Harrow to everyone but family—had made all the arrangements in advance. The embassy car was waiting. Sleek, black, and unassuming, it pulled away with practiced efficiency, weaving them through wide boulevards and narrow alleys until the American embassy came into view. The building loomed like a stately secret, flanked by iron gates, and trimmed hedges.

Inside, they were greeted by a staffer and shown to their rooms in the diplomatic residence. Madison's was tasteful and cold: cream walls, gold trim, antique furniture polished but untouched. It smelled faintly of lavender and history.

She unpacked slowly, deliberate with ritual. Dresses in the wardrobe, shoes in a perfect line by the wall. At home she organized because it was expected. Here she did it because it steadied her — a way to impose order when the room itself meant to be looked at, not lived in.

Nothing here bore a trace of life: no worn armrest, no creak in the floorboards, no hint of someone else's presence. Even in Newport, beneath all the La Croix polish, there was Lucille humming down the hall or Vivienne's scent in passing. This silence had no owner.

She sat at the writing desk, opening a book, but her eyes drifted. Every drawer was empty, as if no one had ever dared to scrawl a letter there. The the tick of a distant clock, the filtered Parisian light through lace curtains — it all pressed her into stillness. She wasn't sure what she was meant to be here. Decoration? A polite shadow for Vivienne?

By the time the knock at her door came, she welcomed it. Even tea, with its etiquette and staging, was better than sitting in a room arranged for show, not for life.

They were escorted to the east salon. Trixie was already seated on a velvet settee near the window, the spring light casting soft shadows across the marble floor. Next to her sat Sabine, the cousin Madison barely remembered—a mannequin on display in a pale blue blouse, hands folded perfectly in her lap.

Madison paused. For an instant, she felt as though she were looking at herself from a few years ago: the same careful posture, the same glassy composure, as if Sabine had been arranged there rather than seated. It unsettled her, the way recognition sometimes does.

"Darling," Trixie said to Madison as they entered, rising with a rustle of silk. "You've grown into a vision."

"I'm afraid the photos don't do you justice," she added, her voice measured but cool. "Though I wish we were meeting under quieter circumstances. Sabine loathes public events, and I suspect your mother only agreed to come because I'm being paraded around like a decorative vase."

Vivienne gave a wry smile, teeth glinting like crystal in sunlight. "If I must endure diplomacy, I prefer it with a flourish."

Madison accepted the air kiss on each cheek with practiced ease, then turned to her cousin, Sabine. "Hello."

Sabine nodded politely. "It's nice to see you again."

Vivienne joined them at the table, settling in with the comfort of someone who belonged. Trixie poured the tea herself, her movements graceful and deliberate, like she'd been rehearsing them for decades. Madison took her cup and sat quietly, watching the room.

Across from her, Sabine looked quietly miserable, her posture perfect but her eyes drifting—bored, uneasy, as if she'd been told to sit still and look pleasant but had long since tuned out. As they sipped their tea, her mother and Trixie eased into conversation like seasoned dancers.

"So," Vivienne said, crossing her legs neatly, "the key to the city. I suppose we'll need to start calling you Madame Paris."

Trixie lifted an eyebrow, amused. "Hardly. But yes, it's a gesture. For contributions to the consular arts, cultural preservation, and 'strengthening Franco-American goodwill.' Their words, not mine."

Vivienne gave a soft hum, setting her teacup down just so. "Still. Quite the resume. Newport hasn't been quite so generous, but Resonance is thriving. We've opened two new satellite programs this year."

Trixie smiled—something small and not entirely warm. "You've always had a talent for visibility."

There was a pause, quiet but not completely uncomfortable. Trixie looked down at her cup, turning it slightly in her hands.

"I miss him, you know," she said at last. "Alaric used to call me when he needed space from the noise. He never said much. Just liked the quiet. I suppose I wasn't very good at giving advice, but I listened."

Vivienne's expression shifted, something softer flickering beneath the polish. "He was good at finding silence when the rest of us couldn't."

Madison watched the shift like a crack in marble. Her mother didn't do softness—not in public, and rarely in private.

Trixie looked up. "How are you holding up?"

Vivienne took her time before answering. "I've found ways to fill the space. Some of them even feel meaningful. Time doesn't heal, exactly—but it dulls the sharp edges."

There was a nod from Trixie—approving, but not indulgent. "Have you ever considered a relationship again?"

The question dropped into the air like a stone. Madison glanced at her mother, surprised to see a flicker of genuine shock in Vivienne's eyes.

"I'm not sure..." Vivienne's voice trailed off.

Trixie turned to Madison with a faint smile. "You know, I introduced your parents. Viv and I were friends long before she and Alaric ever noticed each other. I thought they'd suit. She had the poise he lacked, and he had the warmth she didn't yet know she needed."

Vivienne's face took on a rare tenderness, her eyes drifting somewhere distant. For a moment, she looked not proper, not poised, but young.

"I never knew that," Madison said quietly.

The idea of her mother being introduced to her father by someone else—like a character in a story that began long before she was even imagined—unnerved her. She wasn't sure why. Maybe because it made her mother seem younger, more real. Like someone with secrets Madison hadn't learned yet.

"It's true," Trixie said, pouring a fresh stream of tea. "And should she ever be interested again, I know some wonderful Parisian men—charming, age-appropriate, all terribly discreet."

Vivienne paused, a smile curving her lips as she glanced toward Madison. "Tempting. But I think—for now—I'll pass. This week is all about you."

Trixie smirked and tilted her head toward Vivienne. "We all know better than that, Viv."

They shared a knowing laugh.

Madison sipped her tea and stayed quiet. She had never seen her mother like this—unguarded, almost girlish. Across from her, Sabine still looked uneasy, her smile fragile and forced.

This week would be different.

CHAPTER THIRTY-THREE

The Cousins

The dining room at the American embassy was everything Madison expected—ornate without being gaudy, elegant without feeling lived-in. Crystal chandeliers cast shimmering pools of light over gleaming silverware and polished mahogany. The staff moved like shadows, silent and precise.

Trixie sat at the head of the table, dignified in deep navy, with Charles beside her, smiling in his quiet, diplomatic way. Sabine was dressed to match her mother—poised and tense. Lucian, Sabine's younger brother, fidgeted next to her, tapping a spoon until a glance from Trixie brought him to stillness.

Madison, seated across from her mother, watched the room unfold like a stage play. She wasn't expected to speak much, which suited her. Her French was proficient, but the evening's conversation remained surface-level. Protocols. Guest lists. The phrasing of speeches. It was less a dinner than a press release with appetizers.

Afterward, as the guests trickled out and the staff cleared the last plates, Trixie turned to Vivienne.

"Viv, come out with me," she said lightly. "The city's glowing tonight. Let's take a car and drive along the river, maybe get a drink somewhere. You used to love Paris at night."

Vivienne hesitated, her fingers brushing the rim of her wine glass. "I shouldn't... Madison—"

"She's fine," Trixie said, already standing. "She needs rest more than supervision. And if I don't pry you out of this embassy, I'll never hear the end of it."

Vivienne glanced at Madison, who gave a small shrug. There was no point arguing. Trixie wasn't about to take 'no' for an answer.

"All right," she said. "Just for a bit."

Madison followed them out with her eyes, watching the silhouettes of the two women slip down the corridor—heels clicking, laughter fading as they disappeared.

Left to herself, Madison wandered the hallways for a while before drifting into the library. It was dimly lit, lined with books that smelled old and expensive. She ran a hand along the spines until one caught her eye—a slim volume of French poetry. She took it to a corner armchair, curled her legs beneath her, and began to read.

Sometime later, muffled giggling broke the silence.

She looked up. Footsteps. A stifled laugh. Then Sabine's voice—tight and irritated.

"Lucian, stop it. You're being ridiculous. Just go."

There was a pause. Then another laugh. Madison shifted slightly in her chair, and the sound must've caught their attention. A moment later, two heads peeked around the doorway.

Lucian spotted her first. "Oh," he said, brightening. "Hi."

Sabine sighed but followed him in. "We didn't mean to interrupt."

Madison closed the book around a finger and raised an eyebrow. "It's ok. You can come in."

Lucian hovered behind his sister now as they approached, suddenly too shy to speak. He leaned in and whispered something to Sabine, eyes flicking nervously toward Madison.

Sabine rolled her eyes. "He wants to know what it's like to live in America."

Madison tilted her head slightly. "Probably not much different than here. Just more cars. Less elegance."

Sabine arched a brow. "Do you speak French?"

Madison answered without hesitation, her voice smooth and practiced. "Je parle suffisamment bien pour me débrouiller."

Lucian's eyes widened, clearly impressed. He gave a small nod, still too timid to speak.

Sabine gave a light shrug. "Better than most tourists, though mother would say your accent is too clean. Like you rehearsed it."

Madison shrugged, unbothered.

Sabine glanced toward the doorway, then back. "My mother acts different around your mom. It's weird."

Madison hesitated, then spoke more openly than she expected. "My mother acts differently, too. And your mom—Trixie—she's not what I imagined."

Sabine blinked. "I've never heard anyone call her Trixie before today, not even father."

Madison leaned back slightly, thoughtful. "Sounds like there's a lot we don't know about them."

Sabine nodded. "Clearly."

She sank into the armchair opposite Madison as Lucian circled behind her, lingering without a word now, his presence quiet but attentive.

They spoke for a while after that—about school, music, places they'd visited or wanted to go. Sabine had a dry sense of humor, and Lucian listened more than he spoke, occasionally covering a grin with his hand. At one point, something Sabine said made them both laugh—not politely but actually laugh. The kind that echoed a little in the old embassy room and didn't feel out of place.

Lucian, finally growing more comfortable, leaned forward slightly. His voice was still quiet, but this time he spoke for himself. "Do you have a boyfriend?"

Sabine turned sharply toward him. "Lucian!"

Madison smiled faintly. "No," she said. "I don't."

Lucian grinned, emboldened. "Sabine doesn't either."

Sabine gasped, half scandalized. "Lucian!" Her cheeks flushed as she shot him a glare.

Madison laughed softly. "It's okay," she said, then looked at Lucian with a hint of curiosity. "What about you?"

Lucian hesitated, suddenly quiet again.

Sabine smirked slightly and said a name—softly, almost sing-song. "Chloe."

Lucian's eyes went wide. "She's not my girlfriend!" he blurted, face turning red.

Madison smiled, genuinely amused.

Sabine crossed her arms. "All right, that's enough. It's late."

Lucian groaned. "I'm not even tired."

Sabine tilted her head, her voice warning. "Do I need to bring up Chloe again?"

Lucian scowled but stood up with exaggerated reluctance. "Fine. I'm going."

When he was gone, the room fell quieter. Sabine didn't move right away, and neither did Madison. They kept talking, almost without meaning to. The formality dropped a little more with each passing minute—shared stories about childhood tutors, how their mothers corrected posture with just a glance, the ways they learned to stay quiet in rooms full of adults.

It turned out they had more in common than Madison expected. Enough, at least, to make something feel easy for once. By the time Sabine finally stood to leave, they weren't strangers anymore. They were something new.

Quietly, cautiously, friends.

CHAPTER THIRTY-FOUR

The Key

The morning was cool and bright.

The day of the ceremony arrived with a soft silvery mist still clinging to the edges of the embassy lawn. Madison sat at the vanity in her guest room, hair pinned, dress laid out like armor. The heels were taller than she liked. The makeup was heavier than she needed. But none of that was up for debate.

Vivienne stepped into the doorway without knocking, a sleek silhouette in ivory silk. The softness Madison had seen in Paris these past few days was gone—replaced by the version of her mother she knew best: composed to perfection, every movement rehearsed.

"You look lovely," Vivienne said, walking over and adjusting the clasp on Madison's necklace. "Just remember—there will be cameras. Not just the local press. International outlets. Diplomats. Ambassadors. This is bigger than Newport. Bigger than any Resonance gala."

Madison met her eyes in the mirror, holding back the impulse to roll them. Of course it was. That's why her mother was fixating again.

Vivienne smoothed an invisible wrinkle from Madison's shoulder and stepped back to study her. "Posture. Chin slightly down. Not too much teeth when you smile."

"Yes, mother," Madison murmured.

Vivienne paused. "You only get one impression in these circles, Madison. Don't waste it."

The door clicked shut and Madison exhaled slowly. The day hadn't even started, and already she felt like a product being inspected before shipping.

But she rose, anyway. The shoes hurt. The dress pinched. She smoothed her expression, grabbed her clutch, and walked out the door like she owned the room.

Sabine was waiting outside her door.

"Ready?" she asked, already immaculate in pale blue. Her tone was light, casual. "I thought we could walk over together. They're lining up in the east corridor. It's quicker if we cut through the garden."

They passed through a glass hallway, then out into the crisp morning air. The garden was quiet and clipped, fog still curling around the hedges. Sabine led confidently, heels clicking over the stone path.

A turn. Then another. Then another.

Sabine glanced around, a faint furrow in her brow. "I thought they were meeting us here. This is where they usually gather for events like this."

She paused, then offered, "Let me find one of the embassy staff—make sure we're not in the wrong spot. Just wait here a second, okay?"

Madison waited. A minute passed. Then two. No one came.

Her stomach tightened. The garden, once serene, now felt vast and disorienting.

She finally turned and began walking back the way they'd come, shoes clicking against the stones with growing urgency. She smoothed her dress as she walked, trying to quiet the sick twist in her stomach. It was fine. She'd still be there in time.

After another turn, she spotted a staff member in uniform near a side entrance.

"Excuse me," she said quickly. "I'm supposed to be with the delegation."

The staffer nodded, unfazed. "Right this way, mademoiselle."

By the time Madison was escorted through a side hallway and into the staging corridor, the ceremony had already begun. She could hear applause and camera shutters as she entered.

She stepped into the back of the room just as Trixie took the stage with the mayor, her face bright beneath the lights.

Madison's heels sounded like gunshots across the marble floor. She felt every eye in the room swivel toward her, measuring her lateness, any chance of slipping in unnoticed already gone.

Vivienne wouldn't look at her. She didn't need to.

Madison could feel the disapproval radiating off her like heat.

And Sabine? Already seated. Composed.

After the ceremony, Madison found Sabine near the reception tables, adjusting the place cards one by one, aligning their edges like a puzzle.

"I came back," Sabine said lightly, before Madison could speak. "You were already gone. I assumed you found your way."

Sabine smiled faintly, but her eyes didn't join in.

Madison studied her, seeing through the polish. There was no confusion in Sabine's eyes—only the satisfaction of someone feigning it.

Vivienne passed them without slowing. Not a word. Not a glance. Just the trace of her perfume as she moved down the hall.

Madison just stood there, motionless, as she watched her mother move away from her.

Another camera clicked somewhere off in the distance.

The flight home was silent.

Not a cold war, not exactly. Just cold. Vivienne read a magazine. Madison stared out the window. Somewhere over the Atlantic, she tried once—just once—to speak.

"I didn't mean to be late."

Vivienne didn't look up. "You knew better."

And that was the end of it.

She turned her face back to the window, jaw tight. She had lowered her guard. Trusted someone. And she paid for it.

It wouldn't happen again.

CHAPTER THIRTY-FIVE

The Internship

The room smelled like toner and carpet glue.

It was an afterthought of a space carved out of a larger, more important floor. Beige walls, fluorescent lighting, and three folding chairs made it clear this wasn't about luxury. It was about expedience.

Madison sat with perfect posture in the middle chair, though she hadn't been told to. She hadn't been told anything, really. Her mother had framed it as a "wonderful opportunity" — a phrase Madison had learned to mistrust — and her grandfather's assistant had sent a one-line email: *You'll begin Monday. 8:45 sharp.*

She hadn't asked for this. She didn't want to shadow executives or memorize shipping lanes or attend quarterly reviews. But in the La Croix family, duty was often disguised as privilege — and refusal carried consequences.

To her left, Celeste Whitmore sat upright with rigid composure. Her notebook lay open on the small desk in front of her. Three pens — black, blue, and red — were arranged with the obsessive precision of someone who believed organization was a virtue worth displaying. Her manicure was immaculate; each nail filed to identical length and painted a deep crimson so glossy it looked freshly lacquered.

And on Madison's right: Spencer Hale. All clean lines and practiced manners — the kind who probably wrote his own letter of recommendation. His tie was a little too tight, his hair a little too perfect, but his knee bounced just enough to suggest he wasn't as calm as he pretended. He glanced at her, then quickly looked away — not out of intimidation, Madison noted, but because boys like Spencer didn't know what to do with girls like her.

The silence between them pulsed like an elevator pause.

Then the door creaked open.

Jared Kinney stepped in — mid-thirties, brisk and lean, holding a clipboard. He surveyed them with the satisfaction of someone fulfilling an obligation rather than an interest.

"Welcome to the Summer Internship Program," he said. "You're here because you earned it—through merit, effort, and dedication. Or because your last name opened the right door."

His eyes hovered an extra beat on Madison — the faintest flicker of amusement, as if wondering whether she even knew what "maritime" meant.

She offered a faint, unreadable smile. She had no intention of being ornamental here.

He handed each of them a slim packet of paperwork — confidentiality agreements, emergency contact forms, a printout of the day's agenda. There was also a questionnaire — designed to feel engaging but mostly droll. *What made you interested in this program? Where do you see yourself in five years? What is one personal strength you bring to the workplace?*

"Take a few minutes to fill these out," he said. "Then we'll move on."

The room filled with the rustle of pages and the scratch of pens. Celeste took to the forms like they were a standardized test, racing through them with stiff, mechanical precision. When she finished, she slammed her pen down just loudly enough to declare it. Spencer jumped slightly at the sound, then hunched over his paperwork with renewed urgency, as if he'd fallen behind.

Madison stared at the sheets, pen hovering. Her first instinct was to answer with irony — to write something clever, a small rebellion buried in wit. But she thought better of it. Alastair was watching.

She filled in the blanks with answers that sounded earnest enough. Focused. Curious. Eager to learn. She even underlined a word or two for emphasis. It was almost convincing. She turned the pages with a deliberate slowness, her pen gliding across the lines without urgency, like someone signing autographs at a book launch.

When they finished, another silence settled over the room — thicker this time, heavy with unspoken competition and careful calculation. No one reached for their phone. The scratch of pens had stopped, leaving only the distant hum of the building's ventilation system and the occasional creak of chairs as bodies shifted in the uncomfortable quiet.

Celeste broke first, to no surprise of Madison.

"So... where's everybody going to school next year?" Her tone was casual, but the question was loaded with subtext that everyone in the room understood perfectly. She meant college. She meant rankings and prestige. But more than that, she meant to answer it herself — to establish the benchmark against which the others would be measured.

"I'll start. Georgetown for me," she said, like someone sliding a business card across the table — polished, precise, rehearsed.

Spencer perked up slightly, his shoulders straightening as if he'd been waiting for exactly this opening. "Dartmouth," he said — too quickly, like he was still surprised it was true. Then he cleared his throat and tried again, softening his tone as if to downplay how much it thrilled him just to say it aloud.

Madison knew exactly what the question meant, the careful dance of academic credentials and social positioning. She answered anyway.

"Ashmore," she said, without inflection.

Celeste blinked, then smiled and nodded like that answer made sense.

It didn't.

CHAPTER THIRTY-SIX

The Work Schedule

M adison stared at the schedule.

It wasn't the kind she was used to. A single page. Copied and slightly off-center, as if it had been rushed out at the last minute. Helvetica. All caps. No color to soften it.

She read it the way she always did, measuring the span of time she would be expected to occupy. But this one felt provisional—something put in place to suffice, not to last.

8:45 a.m. – Arrival and Badge Pickup

The badge was card stock, not even laminated. "Intern – M. La Croix." No flourish. Just a barcode and a lanyard that scratched her collarbone.

9:00 a.m. – Welcome

Jared Kinney smiled like it hurt. Used the wrong tone. After the initial paperwork, he spoke for the entire time without really saying anything. She watched his shoes during the welcome speech — cheap leather, over-polished.

9:30 a.m. – Team Introductions

Three interns, ten staff. Only one woman among them — a senior analyst from Compliance, with two silver bracelets that clinked softly whenever she moved. She didn't smile once. Madison liked her immediately.

10:00 a.m. – Departmental Rotation Assignments

Celeste asked if they'd be able to shadow the executive floor. Jared said, "Eventually," in a tone that meant never. He explained they'd start with the basics — logistics, HR, compliance — and rotate weekly. "Exposure breeds understanding," he added, as if quoting a slogan.

10:30 a.m. – Break

No food. No snacks. Just water in cone-shaped paper cups that wilted when they got wet.

10:45 a.m. – Corporate History Slideshow

Spencer took notes. Celeste asked a question she already knew the answer to. Madison watched a light flicker in the corner of the screen — the only honest thing in the room.

11:30 a.m. – "What We Look for in Future Leaders"

A middle manager spoke like he was trying to convince himself. He read the slides to them, word for word. "Initiative. Curiosity. Poise under pressure." Madison mouthed the words with him by the third slide.

12:00 p.m. – Lunch (Cafeteria, 4th Floor)

Build-your-own grain bowls. Celeste asked if the dressing was local. Spencer edged in too close, unaware of how much space he took up. Madison ate quickly and excused herself early.

1:00 p.m. — Shadow: Logistics Team

Numbers, charts, container codes. Spencer lit up. Celeste asked to see the HR side instead. Madison pretended to take notes on the figures, but she was really watching the people—who actually kept the system running, and who didn't.

2:15 p.m. — Personal Branding Session

A young woman with shiny hair and a dead smile told them how to present themselves professionally — posture, diction, what kind of questions to ask in meetings. "You're not just interns," she said. "You're a brand." Madison didn't blink. She'd been branded since birth.

3:00 p.m. — Roundtable: "What Do You Hope to Learn?"

They were told to share aloud. Spencer went first, earnest, and eager. Celeste followed, articulate but theatrical. Madison paused just long enough to make it uncomfortable. Then she smiled and said, "Clarity."

3:30 p.m. — Dismissal and Feedback Cards

Jared asked them to complete anonymous feedback cards. Madison filled in the checkboxes quickly. In the comments section, she wrote: The sessions would benefit from greater concision. She handed it back before he finished explaining how valuable their input was.

On the elevator ride down to the lobby, no one spoke. The lanyard still hung from her neck, and she resisted the urge to remove it. There was something quietly humiliating about the nametag — being reduced to an intern, when she was used to being a La Croix. A lowercase role in an uppercase building.

Celeste shifted beside her, then tilted her head slightly. "La Croix," she said, reading from Madison's badge for the first time all day. "As in... *the* La Croix?"

Madison didn't look at her. "So I've been told."

Spencer blinked and stood a little straighter.

Madison faced the doors and watched her own reflection in the brushed steel.

She wasn't here to make friends, to climb ladders, impress Jared Kinney, or regurgitate keywords like "initiative."

She was here because someone told her she had to be. It wasn't that different from school, really — just quieter, better dressed, and meaner in more polite ways.

But she was already noticing things — not just with the interns, but with the employees. Their names. Who answered questions and who avoided them. Who forced a laugh, and who never made eye contact. The pecking order beneath the polished floor.

Not because she wanted to be part of it. But because some of them — like Jared, like the slideshow guy, and the woman from HR who called her "kiddo" — had all underestimated her. And others still would.

And that was going to be a mistake.

CHAPTER THIRTY-SEVEN

The Executive Floor

I t had been over a week and nothing had changed.

It was the same room. Same folding chairs. Same flickering overhead light. Same stale coffee smell clinging to the carpet like it had always been there.

But today, there was an energy. Not excitement — ambition, maybe. Or nerves dressed as professionalism.

Jared stood at the front again, clipboard in hand, as if the schedule weren't already printed in triplicate. "Good morning," he said, too loudly. "Today you'll each be shadowing a department. Assignments are non-negotiable, so please don't lobby for changes."

Celeste folded her arms. Spencer sat forward like a golden retriever about to be picked for a team.

Madison didn't move.

Jared read from the list.

"Spencer Hale — Logistics. Celeste Whitmore — Marketing. Madison La Croix..." He hesitated.

"...Executive Operations."

The pause wasn't long, but it said everything. Heads turned. Madison kept her eyes on the clipboard like it was just another line item.

Her shoulders drew back a fraction, posture straightening as if by habit. She didn't smile. Not yet.

Someone exhaled — sharp and disbelieving, like a laugh swallowed too late.

Jared didn't explain. He just checked a box and moved on.

Madison knew what they were thinking. That she was getting special treatment. That "Executive Operations" was code for a corner office babysitting assignment.

They weren't entirely wrong.

This was nepotism. Pure and polished. But it wasn't a gift. It was a test.

Her grandfather hadn't spoken to her directly about it. He didn't need to. But the implication was clear: *impress me again.*

She had done it once already — at the gala, when the room had been full of preening and she, alone, had stood still enough for the spotlight to find her.

But Alastair hadn't judged on a single dance. He had been watching for years — watching them both.

August had been the obvious choice once, but indulgence had dulled him. While he chased attention, she drew it. Where he sought approval, she created it.

Alastair had seen the difference.

So, this wasn't a favor. It wasn't even an experiment. It was succession, under glass.

At the top floor, a woman at reception glanced at Madison's badge, then pressed a button under the desk. The door clicked open.

She stepped into a space that didn't smell like the intern area. It smelled like paper and leather and whatever cologne had settled into the walls over the decades. No one greeted her.

She found him in the boardroom — not seated, but standing at the window with one hand in his pocket and the other resting on the back of a leather chair. He didn't turn around when she entered.

"You wore navy," he said, still looking out the windows.

Madison straightened slightly. She had worn navy, with cream trim and buttons that didn't gleam. Understated. Serious. Intentional.

When he did turn, he didn't greet her. He just looked her over — the way he had at the family gathering years ago. An appraisal. Then a pause.

He nodded once, then spoke to the empty room: "Better posture than most of the associates."

It landed the way he meant it to — a challenge disguised as praise.

She didn't speak. Not yet. Her throat was dry, even if no one could tell.

But inside, she felt like she was ten again. In new shoes with bows that hadn't been broken in, pretending she wasn't terrified of the old man with impossible standards.

But her expression stayed even.

She could play this part.

He checked his watch, then looked at her again.

"You'll sit in on the 10:30. Don't speak. If you're bored, take notes."

He turned back toward the window.

"They think I brought you up here to humor you," he said. "They're wrong."

Madison opened her mouth. "Yes, gran—" She caught herself. Straightened.

"Understood, Mr. La Croix."

She couldn't see his face, but his posture shifted — just slightly. Almost as if he smiled.

Almost.

CHAPTER THIRTY-EIGHT

The Board Meeting

The room was colder than she expected — not in temperature, but in tone.

Nine men. One woman. All seated before she entered. No one stood.

Alastair didn't introduce her. He gestured to an empty chair near the end of the long table and simply said, "Observe."

Chairs shifted. Not in welcome, but in acknowledgement of the order. She sat, spine straight, eyes level. A few glanced at her—curiosity on one face, dismissal on most. A joke passed down the table, half-heard. Someone smirked. No one explained.

They spoke in code. "Restructure," "positioning," "margin correction." She understood just enough to follow, not enough to contribute. That wasn't the point. The point was the cadence. Who interrupted. Who rephrased. Who yielded — and who didn't.

Graham Ellison, one of the few senior executives Madison recognized by name, spoke sparingly. But each time he did, the room adjusted around him. Alastair never once cut him off. That told her more than anything Graham actually said.

One of the younger board members tried to challenge a proposal — something about consolidating overseas operations. Alastair didn't raise his voice. He simply looked up from his notes, met the man's eye, and said, "noted." Some papers shuffled. The topic died.

Later, an older director circled back to a phrase already drained of meaning. "Brand integrity." Alastair clicked his pen once. Eyes slid to Graham. Graham didn't move. The silence that followed carried more force than rebuttal.

The lone woman leaned forward, finally speaking: a number, a date, a name. No abstractions. The table went still. Alastair let her finish.

Madison observed, as she was told. The real power in the room wasn't in who talked the most. It was in who could end a conversation without effort.

The boardroom emptied slowly, leaving behind only the quiet scrape of chairs and the scent of coffee that had long gone cold.

Alastair remained seated. Madison stood, unsure whether to stay or follow the others. Before she could decide, a voice entered the room.

"Still breathing?"

It was Graham.

He walked in without fanfare, no notebook, no agenda, just a glance exchanged with Alastair — the kind that didn't need context.

"Sit," Alastair said, gesturing not to Madison, but to the chair beside him. Madison stayed where she was.

Graham took his seat, exhaled, and leaned back. "They're nervous," he said. "And when they get nervous, they talk too much."

Madison listened. This was the part they never put in the reports.

"They should be nervous," Alastair replied. "Vireon is circling."

"They're circling everyone," Graham said.

Madison thought this Vireon sounded like vultures — circling something half-alive, waiting for the moment it stopped pretending.

Graham spoke again. "They've got teeth. And cash. We're not exactly unified."

Alastair didn't argue. He turned to Madison.

"Do you know what Vireon does?"

She nodded slowly and repeated some of the words she overheard in the meeting. "Tech. Acquisitions. Influence."

Alastair's mouth twitched. "They made a move on the dock contracts last quarter. Soft pressure. Nothing serious."

"They'll try again," Graham added. "Probably during the festival. That's how they work. Timing, visibility, spectacle. They'll want a big press release — cameras, donors, ribbon-cutting optics."

Alastair gave a faint grunt. "Of course they will. We're not the only ones who care about *brand integrity*," he said, tone just edged enough to sting.

Graham gave a short grin, the kind that didn't need to last to be real.

But Madison noticed it. It was a side of her grandfather she hadn't seen before — dry, deliberate, even a little playful. Almost like something her father might've said. The thought flickered and was gone, but the impression lingered.

Madison sat back in her chair. These were the conversations no intern got to hear.

She wasn't fully welcome. But she was still in the room.

And for now, that was enough.

By late afternoon, she was back in the first-floor conference room. Same chairs. Same stale air.

But the silence was heavier now. Spencer slouched like he'd spent the day being talked at — container codes, distribution schedules, numbers that blurred the longer he stared. Celeste's polish was intact, but her eyes were sharp, restless; she'd been parked in a marketing bullpen, handed a deck to flip through, and told little that mattered.

Madison's posture was composed, almost deliberate. She had been in the boardroom. She hadn't spoken, of course — but she'd heard everything. Strategy, risk, timing. No intern got that close.

Spencer glanced over at Madison, quick but curious, like he was still trying to reconcile her blazer with her age. Celeste didn't bother to hide it. She stared openly, as if measuring Madison against a résumé no one else had seen.

"All right," Jared said, cutting across the silence. He handed out feedback forms — a stack of printed sheets with lines for reflection.

What did you learn today? What stood out? What could have been improved?

Celeste began writing immediately, in long, looping script. Spencer frowned and tapped his pen like he wanted to get it right.

Madison took a single sheet.

She didn't write what she learned. She wrote what they'd shown her. Two words.

Brand Integrity.

CHAPTER THIRTY-NINE

The Officers' Club

The envelope was heavy with pretense.

The invitation arrived at their residence sealed with the La Croix crest, though it hardly needed formality. When Alastair said attendance was expected, attendance was guaranteed. Madison read the embossed card with detached interest, noting the location — the Newport Officers' Club — and the guest list full of names she only half recognized. It would be, as her grandfather said, a "gathering of industry minds." She knew better. It was another performance.

Vivienne had already begun talking about the dinner days in advance. "It'll be good for Resonance to be seen supporting events like this," she said, already rehearsing how it might play in future press releases. Madison didn't argue. She didn't have the energy.

The night before the event was filled with dread. The thought of slipping into another evening of well-aged men and barely concealed power games was exhausting. And doing so with Vivienne?

Excruciating.

The Officers' Club was dressed in white linens and glinting crystal, the lighting mellow and antique, as though the room itself disapproved of anything built after 1955. Servers moved like ghosts between the tables, offering flutes of champagne before the first course. Alastair stood near the fireplace with a circle of suits, all talking with the kind of ease that came from inherited relevance.

Vivienne arrived late, fashionably, in a pale green gown that skimmed her frame and drew just enough attention to remind people she still had it. Madison, in a black column dress and low chignon, kept her posture perfect and her expression unreadable. She scanned the room.

Aunt Mattie took her usual place near the front of the room, regal in navy silk and seated beside a shipping magnate she probably disliked but tolerated with dry charm. She spotted Madison once and raised a glass subtly, offering silent approval that meant more than anything spoken.

August was also there, already bored and tugging at his cuffs. With few girls his age in attendance, there was no one to impress and nothing to anchor his attention. He looked adrift — the kind of restlessness that always made him either sulk or meddle. If he tried to speak to her tonight, she'd find an excuse to disappear.

Graham Ellison stood further off, hands behind his back, offering quiet nods but rarely words. A few others lingered at cocktail tables or leaned into conversations she didn't recognize — older men in suits, all equally forgettable.

Her eyes moved lazily across the room, scanning for something — anything — that might break the monotony. That's when she saw him. At one table toward the back, there was a boy. He looked about Madison's age — maybe sixteen, seventeen at most — wearing a suit that didn't quite fit but with posture that tried to make up for it. He wasn't talking. He was watching. Her.

Not the way old men watched. Not how August looked at other girls. Not like inventory. This was something more uncertain. Something closer to wonder.

She didn't know his name. But the look, that part she knew. She'd seen it in school hallways, in awkward donors' sons at fundraisers. She smiled faintly and looked away.

As the minutes dragged on, she found herself glancing around the room, and each time her eyes returned to him, he was still watching. Not openly. He looked away quickly whenever they made eye contact, feigning interest in his drink or the conversation beside him. But the pattern repeated itself enough to confirm it wasn't accidental.

Halfway through the second course, a folded square of white paper appeared on her bread plate. She glanced across the room and saw a nervous flicker of movement — the boy looking down too quickly.

She opened it under the table.

Out back. Five minutes. I just want to say
hello.

Madison stared at it for a moment. She was bored. Vivienne was beside her, name-dropping producers no one in
the room cared about. Alastair was still playing godfather
at the fireplace. Aunt Mattie was nowhere to be seen.

Vivienne didn't even look up — too absorbed in her
story to notice Madison pushing back her chair. Without
ceremony, Madison rose and slipped out quietly, the hem
of her dress brushing past the leg of the table like a whispered exit.

Not because she had any motive. Not because she cared
who he was. But because, for once, something unpre-
dictable had entered the room.

And that, at least, was interesting.

CHAPTER FORTY

The Meeting

Madison stepped into the night air with a practiced calm.

The club's back terrace was quiet — dimly lit, ringed with trimmed hedges and the distant murmur of waves. She walked along the stone path, heels tapping softly, until she rounded the corner.

The boy stood when he saw her. Too quickly. As if he doubted that she would really come. His expression lit up — flattered, nervous, hopeful.

"Hello," he said, brushing his palms against his slacks.

She gave him a polite smile. "Hello." Then pivoted to go, like that was all he'd earned.

"Wait—"

She paused, glanced back. "Your note said you just wanted to say hello."

That made him laugh, unexpectedly. "Yeah, well... I couldn't write everything that I wanted to say on a napkin."

She arched an eyebrow and gave a coy grin.

"Come on. You looked just as bored as I did," he added. "I thought maybe you wanted to breathe for a minute. Or talk... maybe."

She said nothing at first. She just studied him. He was handsome in a soft, uncertain way — like someone still growing into his own features. Then he said:

"Please."

That word — delicate, real — was enough. So, she stayed.

And they talked. Or rather, he did.

He introduced himself — Evan Chambers. Said he didn't live here, just flew in for the dinner because his father was a partner at Vireon. That mattered. Madison didn't let it show.

He offered up stories about his school, his summer plans, and the dinner inside. He wasn't trying to impress with charm or status — just hoping she might find him interesting. And strangely, she did.

He was earnest, awkward in a gentle way, and didn't once fawn over her looks or step over the line. It was disarming. Refreshing, even.

She let him talk, offering a smile here, a nod, a small laugh. She mentioned that her mother was here with Resonance, doing some fundraising. It was enough to keep him going — still eager, still flattered, still leaning toward her like he couldn't quite believe she hadn't walked away yet.

"My dad's actually working on something with the harbor," he said, clearly trying to sound impressive. "Trying to get it done before the festival. Should be a big announcement if it happens."

Madison tilted her head, curious but not overly probing. "The Mariner's Festival?"

"Yeah. I guess it's a big deal."

She nodded slowly. "It is."

They talked a while longer — nothing pressing, nothing rehearsed. He asked if she liked school, and she offered the kind of answers that kept the conversation moving but gave nothing away. He talked about his life out west, how he might study economics or law, how he wasn't sure yet.

She listened. He wasn't posturing — he was just uncertain and trying. She could see how much he wanted her to like him, but not in the usual way. Not with performance. Just with hope.

He looked nervous all of a sudden, like the courage it took to speak might vanish if he didn't use it quickly. "Would it be all right if I saw you again sometime? I mean... if you wanted to."

"I'm not sure," she said, turning over how that could even work. "I thought you lived out of town."

"Well, my dad's going to be back in town in two weeks for that deal," he said quickly. "Maybe I could come with him. If not, then I know we'll be back for the festival."

She smiled. "Okay, I'd like that."

He looked stunned, like he hadn't expected her to say yes.

She took a pen from her clutch and scribbled her number on the back of his note. "Call me," she said, handing it back. "If your schedule changes."

Then she turned and walked back inside, shoes clicking softly against the stone. He didn't move. He just stood there in stunned silence, staring down at the slip of paper in his hands like it had changed the shape of his evening — maybe even something more.

She returned to her seat beside her mother, who hadn't seemed to notice that she'd left. Vivienne was still mid-anecdote, gesturing with one hand, nodding emphatically at someone across the table. Madison smoothed her dress, picked up her water glass, and let the noise settle around her like fog. Her mind was still outside.

Evan had actually been... nice. He didn't fixate on her looks, didn't push for attention or validation. A little self-congratulatory, yes — but not in the calculating way she was used to. More like someone unsure of what mattered and offered everything just in case. But it wasn't the boasting that stayed with her.

It was what he chose to share.

A Vireon deal. In two weeks. Before the festival.

That was what they had been discussing in the board meeting. Graham had said they still didn't know Vireon's timeline. And Evan Chambers had just given it up without even asking who she was.

Her grandfather would want to know.

CHAPTER FORTY-ONE

The Mariner's Festival: Opening

All of Newport seemed to hum with anticipation.

The Mariner's Festival was more than just a weekend of sails and seafood — it was the city's defining ritual. Streets were being swept, storefronts redecorated, flags unfurled. Yacht clubs polished their brass, local designers released limited-run collections, and even the skeptical old guard had their suits pressed.

For families like the La Croix, the festival was part legacy, part performance. Alastair, of course, served as Grand Marshal, a role he wore like an epaulet. Madison had grown up beneath its shadow — parades, speeches, photo calls, carnivals that filled the waterfront with lights and music. But this year felt different. Bigger. Hungrier.

Everyone wanted something. A donation, a quote, a favor, a seat. Even those pretending to be above it were subtly circling the center. Madison could see it clearly now. The festival wasn't about tradition. It was about positioning.

That was why the timing mattered.

She had passed along what the boy had said — first to her grandfather. Alastair said little at the time, but the next morning Graham was in the drawing room with a notepad and two phones. A Vireon deal, scheduled to close just before the festival. Quietly, the La Croix's moved first. Graham made calls. Alastair leaned on old debts. In less than a week, they'd secured a competing deal of their own — not larger, but earlier. Vireon had money. La Croix had timing.

By the time Vireon's press team issued their carefully worded announcement, the docks had already been spoken for. It wasn't sabotage. Simply better execution.

At a luncheon the day before the festival, with city officials and press seated at long white tables beneath a sailcloth tent, Alastair raised his glass for a toast. "To initiative," he said, voice clear, hand steady.

"And the future," he added.

His head didn't turn. But Madison would have sworn — just for a second — his eyes flicked in her direction.

She didn't smile. But she felt something in her chest. Pride rose within her, quiet and certain, like the tide coming in.

Madison and Evan had spoken on the phone several times since the dinner. Nothing structured, nothing daily — just the kind of conversations that slipped into place when the timing worked. He didn't get to come back for the harbor deal — probably for the better, given how it all went down — but he was planning to be in town for the festival.

He couldn't wait.

She had more on her plate for the festival than she liked to admit. Ashmore obligations, Resonance appearances, and maybe — if someone required it — a brief appearance on behalf of the company. Her calendar was already crowded. But there were gaps. And Evan wanted as many of them as he could get.

What surprised Madison most was how close they'd gotten over the phone. They weren't alike — not even close. He went to public school in California, didn't wear a uniform, had never heard of Ashmore. He called sneakers "shoes" without irony. East Coast and West Coast, polish and plain. But maybe that was what she liked about him.

His life felt simpler. Not easy, but real. He talked about things without wrapping them in language. Asked questions without pretense. Even if his father was an executive at a major tech company, Evan didn't act like a prince of anything. And for once, Madison didn't feel like she had to perform.

She wouldn't admit it aloud — not to her mother, not to Abigail or Lydia, not even to herself if pressed — but she was kind of looking forward to seeing him again. Not because he dazzled her. But because he didn't try to.

That alone felt rare.

The festival opened with the usual fanfare: a cannon fired from the harbor, sailboats cutting across the bay in tight formation, and the mayor declaring the weekend officially underway with an overly long speech that no one actually listened to. Tourists gathered along the docks, children held balloon animals, and camera crews jockeyed for footage of city council members pretending to enjoy chowder.

Madison had seen it all before, but this year, she was being watched. She'd been watched before, of course — that came with the last name. But those moments had been ceremonial, more for show than scrutiny. This time, it was different. The attention was sharper, quieter. And it came from people who actually mattered.

Evan's first chance to see her would come after the family's Saturday brunch — one of those semi-obligatory gatherings with too many cousins and not enough coffee. Vivienne would float around trying to seem both central and above it, though she carried an air of quiet expectancy this year. Trixie had arrived from Paris, all warm cheek kisses and diplomatic charm, drifting through the room like she still belonged to all of it.

Madison was seated beside Aunt Mattie, who was already on her second mimosa. Across the table sat Sabine, offering polite smiles that Madison returned with a kind of curated indifference. There was no open tension —

just the kind of chilly civility that came from unfinished business.

Sometime midway through brunch, Aunt Mattie's gaze drifted past the crowd and out toward the sidewalk. "That blazer is about half a size too hopeful," she murmured, lifting her glass slightly. Madison followed her line of sight.

Evan was just outside the open-air terrace, standing near the stone path, hands tucked into the pockets of a navy blazer that didn't quite fit his shoulders yet. He wasn't pacing, just standing still, scanning the tables, hoping to spot her.

Madison hadn't touched her croissant. But she was more awake now. And curious. She suppressed a smile, but something in her posture shifted — a bit straighter, a little brighter.

"Mm-hmm," Mattie said, the corner of her mouth tugging upward. "Some poor boy wanders in wearing ambition and suddenly someone's spine remembers it has options."

Madison glanced sideways, her expression somewhere between amused and unbothered, one brow raising just enough to register the point.

Mattie sipped her drink. "What are you waiting for? He's a better use of your morning than this gallery of fork-clinking genealogy."

Madison smiled — not wide, but enough — and rose from her chair with the kind of grace that made it look like she'd never intended to stay long anyway. She slipped away without a word.

She didn't look back.

CHAPTER FORTY-TWO

The Mariner's Festival: The Tell

They didn't make a plan, exactly.

Evan was just there — on the lawn, by the Ferris wheel, near the bandstand — whenever Madison's obligations gave her a moment to breathe. Between photo ops and brunches and charity check-ins, she found him again and again.

They sat on benches sticky with salt air and powdered sugar. They wandered the carnival, eating things she normally wasn't allowed to touch — fried dough, something served on a stick, a lemon ice that turned her lips blue.

They crammed into one of the photo booths near the end of the pier, the kind with the scratchy curtain and smudged mirror. The photos came out in a crooked strip

— her trying not to smile, him grinning like he'd stumbled on something valuable and didn't want to jinx it.

He made faces when she posed for photos and once did an exaggerated bow from the crowd when her name was called on stage. She scolded him after, pulled him aside and hissed that he couldn't do that. But she was laughing when she said it.

It wasn't like her. But she didn't mind.

It brought back echoes of the boy from Resonance — back when she'd been younger, more naive. But she wasn't that girl anymore. This felt steadier. Safer. Like something she could choose, not fall into.

Evan didn't rush. He didn't push. He asked if she was tired. If she'd eaten. If she wanted to leave.

She always said no. She didn't want to miss any of it.

The week moved like that — in stretches and skips. Formal by day, wandering by dusk. And through it all, he stayed right at the edges. Not chasing. Not clinging. Just waiting for when she had time again.

And somehow, she always did.

It was the next-to-the-last day of the festival.

Evan steered her in the direction of the docks. "Do you like boats?"

Madison blinked, then gave the faintest smile. "I do."

"They're running the harbor ferry every half hour," he said. "We could take a ride. Just for the view."

She surprised herself with how quickly she said yes.

At the edge of the dock, she slipped off her shoes and carried them in her hand. The planks were cool beneath her feet. Evan noticed, but didn't ask.

The ferry was small, paint flaking at the corners, its wooden seats scuffed and worn. They found a spot near the stern. As the ropes were loosened and the boat began to pull away, Madison leaned forward.

Just beyond the inlet bobbed the red buoy, leaning slightly to one side. She stood, lifted her hand in a mock salute, crisp and certain.

Evan followed her gaze. "What are you doing?"

"It's for Sir Reginald," she said matter-of-factly. "Guardian of the bay. My father made me salute him every time we went out. Said he'd never let a scoundrel through."

Evan grinned. "And you still do it?"

"Some habits stick." Her eyes stayed on the buoy as it slid past, her voice softer now.

The hum of the motor filled the quiet. She hesitated, then added, "He used to tell me stories out here. Pirates, treasure, dolphins that brought luck. Most of it was non-sense, but I believed every word."

Her fingers tightened around her shoes. "Out here, I never felt like I had to be anyone but myself."

She stopped there, startled at how much she'd shared. The words hung between them, fragile as glass.

Evan didn't press. He only nodded, steady as the water beneath them. "That makes sense."

And somehow, it did.

When they returned to shore, they found a quiet bench behind the carousel, the kind that sat just slightly uneven on the bricks. A paper tray of fries sat between them. Madison picked at them absently, salt clinging to her fingertips, while Evan watched with the kind of soft amusement that didn't ask for anything. Like seeing her do something ordinary made the entire day feel rare.

He let the silence linger, content, before finally speaking.

"I don't have to be back early tonight," he said, then paused. "Was thinking maybe... a movie? Or just—stay out a little longer. If you're allowed."

She smiled faintly. "Allowed, huh? That depends who you ask."

"Then maybe don't ask," he said. His grin was easy, almost boyish. "Anyway, my dad's tied up at some late-night thing down by the docks tonight. He didn't seem thrilled."

Madison looked up. "At the docks? At night?"

"Yeah, I thought it was kind of weird. But he said not to wait up."

Evan said it like it didn't matter, like it was background noise that gave him more time with her. But to Madison, it stood out—like a dropped pin marking something she shouldn't ignore.

She didn't answer right away. Just stole another fry and looked out toward the carnival.

She was torn now. The idea of staying out later—of not having to watch the time—felt like something rare and stolen. But her mind also fixated on what Evan had said. A late-night meeting at the docks. Was Vireon up to something?

She didn't want to think about that. Not tonight. Not with him. She wanted the extra time. She wanted freedom.

But she kept hearing echoes from the boardroom, clipped phrases from Graham, reminders of what could be lost by letting their guard down.

Her hand paused halfway to the tray. Just for a second.

Then she sighed, just audibly enough to register, and turned to him with practiced regret. "That actually sounds perfect," she said. "But I just remembered—I have something I can't miss."

Evan's smile faltered. "Oh. Okay."

"But I can meet you later," she added quickly. "Maybe in a couple of hours?"

He nodded, clearly disappointed, but didn't press.

She stood quickly, brushing salt from her skirt, and gave him the briefest smile. "I'll find you later," she said, already stepping away.

By the time she turned the corner, she was practically running.

Madison burst into her grandfather's study without knocking, startling him. He was standing by the window, rehearsing the closing remarks for the festival ceremony, half-memorized note cards fanned out in one hand. He turned, visibly thrown.

"There needs to be an emergency board meeting," she said, her tone sharper than she expected.

He studied her for a moment, then turned to his assistant. "Half an hour. Full board."

The conference room buzzed with confusion. Voices rose and fell in frustration. "Why are we here?" one asked. "What's the urgency?"

Alastair didn't answer right away. When the room quieted, he leaned back in his chair and gestured to Madison.

"I didn't call this meeting," he said. "She did."

Outrage followed.

"She's a child."

"This is ridiculous."

"You can't be serious."

Alastair's response was calm. "All noted." He turned to Madison. "You have the floor."

She stood; shoulders squared. "Vireon's not finished. There's a meeting tonight at the docks. Quiet, off-the-record. Desperate."

Someone scoffed. "And how do you know this?"

Graham leaned forward, interrupting. "Who cares? If it's true, we might be looking at leverage. If anything illegal is happening—bribery, tampering, whatever—we might be able to expose it. If we make the right call, Vireon's off the docks. For good."

He was already pulling out his phone.

The room fell into murmurs and shuffling.

And this time, Alastair didn't hide his expression. He looked at Madison and smiled—truly smiled.

It was the first time she'd ever seen it.

CHAPTER FORTY-THREE

The Mariner's Festival: More than a Little

The lights of the festival had thinned.

Families were already home. The Ferris wheel creaked through its last slow turn, casting long shadows over the boardwalk. Madison walked quietly through it all, jacket pulled around her shoulders, the echo of her heels softened by the sea air.

She found Evan near the edge of the main square, just beyond the games and food stalls, where the noise started to dissolve into the hum of the harbor. Evan was leaning against a lamppost, hands in his pockets, watching the carousel wind down for the night. When he saw her, he stood straighter, his expression sharpening.

"I wasn't sure you'd make it," he said.

"I said I would."

They didn't hug. But she nudged his shoulder slightly. "Still feel like seeing a movie?"

He smiled. "More than anything."

They walked to the small theater just off the main street. The marquee was half-lit, the sidewalk quiet. They bought tickets from a bored teenager who didn't look up once. Inside, the lobby smelled like butter and musty carpet.

Madison pointed to the screen. "Have you seen this one?"

He grinned. "Nope."

She smiled. "I have. The book's better. But I'll try not to compare it out loud.

"You can if you want."

They sat, not too close, but not too far. As the movie began, Madison recited lines under her breath, almost unaware she was doing it. Evan didn't stop her. He wasn't watching the movie. He was watching her watch it.

About halfway through, she caught him smiling.

"What?" she asked, eyes still on the screen.

"Nothing." He hesitated. "Just—you really like the story. I can tell."

She glanced at him. "It's dumb."

"Maybe. But you lit up when it started."

They went quiet again. She didn't move her hand when it brushed against his.

Later, when the credits rolled and the room filled with soft light, Madison stretched and looked over at him.

"So?" she asked. "Did you like it?"

He nodded. "It was great."

She raised an eyebrow. "You watched *me* the entire time."

"That was the best part."

She rolled her eyes, stood, and pulled on her jacket. "Alright, charmer. Come on."

They stepped outside into the night, the theater door clicking shut behind them.

They walked in silence, streetlamps casting a soft, amber glow.

"Hey," he said, finally. "I like you, Madison. Like... I really like you."

She stared ahead, jaw tight. Her first instinct was to make a joke, to deflect. But the look on his face stopped her.

After a beat, she sighed. "I kind of like you too."

He smiled — not triumphant, just content.

She glanced at him sideways, almost smiling at herself. "Just a little," she added because she had to keep things level.

They didn't kiss. They didn't hold hands. But she didn't move away either.

Outside, the wind shifted off the water, and somewhere in the distance, the last of the carnival lights went dark.

They lingered a moment longer under the lamplight, neither ready to end it.

"I can't believe tomorrow's the last day," Evan said.

"I know." Madison's voice was quiet. "It went too fast."

"Will I see you?"

She hesitated. "I have another family brunch."

He made a face. "Of course you do."

"But I'll be free after."

He smiled, softer now. "Then after it is."

They stood there another minute, neither quite sure what to say next. Then Madison gave a small nod, turned, and walked back into the quiet night.

It wasn't until she was alone—past the harbor, past the thinning crowds—that she let herself feel it. Not quite joy, not exactly. But something remarkably close.

Then she smiled. The real kind.

CHAPTER FORTY-FOUR

The Choice

The last day of a festival feels hollow.

Boats rocked listlessly in their slips, flags limp and tired against their poles. Banners came down in slow folds, volunteers working with the efficiency of undertakers. The smell of funnel cakes still clung to the breeze, more memory than promise — sweetness fading into the catalogue of things that once were.

The terrace buzzed with the subdued energy of an event winding down, conversations peppered with "next year" and "what a lovely time" in the cadence of social obligations fulfilled. Madison arrived late. Not enough to cause a stir or draw disapproval, but enough for Aunt Mattie to notice.

She was sipping something citrusy from a crystal glass as Madison took her seat beside her. "You must've made an impression on your grandfather," Mattie said, her voice carrying a blend of amusement and gentle provocation. "He wasn't in a foul mood for once. I thought I saw the corners of his mouth lift when you arrived. Either the ghost of a smile or a facial tic. Hard to say."

Madison didn't answer. Her attention was already elsewhere. She was scanning the area around the terrace. Evan wasn't there.

He didn't appear during the first course. Or the second. Laughter felt forced, second helpings unwanted. Madison found herself checking her watch with the frequency of someone waiting for a verdict.

When brunch finally ended, she stood quickly, eyes already sweeping the crowd again. But before she could slip through the maze of dispersing guests, Mattie linked her arms with casual intent.

"I think I'll walk with you," she announced. "Whatever maneuver you pulled off to make Alastair look almost human, I want the full report — preferably before that young magician shows up and makes you vanish in a cloud of mystique."

Madison exhaled through her nose. There was no point in arguing.

As they walked through the garden, past beds of roses that perfumed the air with their dying sweetness, Madison spotted him.

Evan stood across the gravel path, positioned just beyond the main cluster of departing festival-goers. His usual easy posture was gone, replaced by something rigid and defensive. His expression was tense, jaw set in a way that made him look older than he was.

Mattie saw him too, and more importantly, she saw Madison's reaction. "That one looks like he came for answers. Brace yourself, Maddie."

Madison crossed over to him with slow, measured steps. She stopped just short of him.

"Hey," she said, the word emerging with a forced calm.

Evan's familiar smile was gone. "Where did you go yesterday afternoon?" his voice carrying an edge she had never heard before.

"What do you mean?" Madison replied, a stalling tactic.

Evan swallowed hard. "My dad. He found our photo. From the photo booth. He knew who you were. About your family."

Madison's jaw tightened, but she stayed quiet.

"He said you were using me," Evan continued, his voice growing shakier with each word. "That you were feeding your grandfather information. That the deal at the docks was sabotaged because of me. That I'd been stupid."

She looked at him, unblinking. Her face a blank canvas that revealed nothing of the storm building inside of her. "And what do you think?"

"I want to believe it wasn't like that," he said, the hope in his voice nearly breaking her resolve. "That you actually like me."

The festival noise—distant laughter—blurred into background. The world narrowed to this moment, this crossroads where everything she had been taught collided with everything she actually wanted.

"Was any of it real?" he asked, his voice barely above a whisper.

Her heart was screaming yes. Her throat burned with the words she wanted to say. That every laugh had been genuine, every smile authentic, that it was more real than anything else in her carefully orchestrated life.

She wanted to grab his hand, to explain the impossible position she had been placed in, to apologize for every piece of truth she hadn't been able to offer. That she really did like him, far more than the casual "little" she had teasingly admitted. Way more than was safe or smart or strategically sound.

But she couldn't. Her training ran deeper than desire. Taught from birth to protect the brand more than anything else—even at the cost of something that might have been enduring.

Her gaze slipped toward the gravel at her feet, focusing on the intricate pattern of stones as if they could offer sanctuary from the weight of his expectation. Her breath caught in her chest, a small betrayal of the emotion she was fighting to contain.

"No," she said, the single syllable falling between.

The word hit him like a slap. He searched her face desperately, looking for some crack in her resolve, some trace of the girl he thought he had gotten to know over the last few weeks. The shared conversations, the easy laughter, the magic of discovery—it couldn't have all been performance. It couldn't have been nothing.

"Really?" he asked, and the disbelief in his voice cut deeper than anger would have.

She didn't answer, couldn't trust herself to speak again without everything spilling out in a torrent. Instead, her eyes traced the lines in the pavement as if they could offer a map to somewhere safer, somewhere she could rest her thoughts.

He blinked once, slowly, like someone waking from a dream they wished could continue. "Okay," he said, the word heavy with finality. Then he turned and walked away without looking back.

She didn't cry. But she wanted to—wanted to let the tears fall, wanted to call after him, wanted to take back the lie that had probably destroyed the first thing she'd let herself believe in for years.

Aunt Mattie had positioned herself close enough to hear the entire exchange. She let Madison stand in the heavy silence for several long seconds before stepping up beside her.

"That boy," she said with pointed deliberation, "looked at you the way your father used to look at Vivienne before he forgot how. Like how your uncle Harry still looks at me, even now."

Madison didn't move though the words landed with calculated precision.

"I saw you," Mattie continued relentlessly, her tone gentle but unyielding. "Every time someone walked by outside, every time a door opened, your eyes went straight there. You were looking for him with the kind of hope that most people spend their whole lives trying to find."

The silence stretched between them.

"You want to be Alastair? Your mother? Fine," Mattie said, her voice carrying a mixture of disappointment and challenge. "But don't pretend you don't have a choice in the matter. Don't convince yourself that this is just how things are."

Madison said nothing in response, couldn't find words for the complexity of what she was feeling. She nodded just once, a small gesture of acknowledgment, and walked away.

She knew she wasn't Alastair, with his cold pragmatism that put business before everything else. She wasn't Vivienne, either, with her elegant desperation and charm as a substitute for anything genuine.

But Mattie was absolutely right about the most important thing: she did have a choice.

She could chase after him right now, confess what she felt, step out from behind the scaffolding of family expectations and let herself be seen as she truly was. She could risk security for the possibility of something real.

Or she could stay safely shielded behind the mask that had protected her for so long—smile for the next photo opportunity, master the next social obligation, and take her predetermined place in the family's polished wall of legacy.

Her last memory of her father resurfaced—that morning when she had been too proud, too stubborn to reach for him when he had tried to connect. She had thought there would be more time. There wasn't.

The weight of that truth pressed down on her now, dense and unyielding. The window for opportunity was

narrowing with every breath, every second she stood between what was safe and what was true.

In the distance, she could see Evan's retreating figure,
growing smaller with each step, soon to disappear entirely
into the crowd of departing guests and lost chances.

So she made her choice.

And it cost her everything.

THE END

Acknowledgements

This book took shape over a long stretch of time, and it would not exist without a small number of people who offered clarity, patience, and honest insight when it mattered.

Thank you to my daughter Sarah for creating the cover and giving the book its face. Many thanks to my daughter-in-law Sarah, who served as the primary editor, reading the manuscript closely and offering thoughtful, direct guidance that helped shape it along the way.

Thank you as well to my wife and my mother-in-law for reading early drafts and sharing their candid reactions. Their willingness to say what worked—and what didn't—made the book stronger.

Finally, thank you to the readers who choose to spend their time here. I hope the story rewards your attention.

Discussion Questions

1. **Madison grows up surrounded by expectations about family, status, and legacy.**
   In what ways do these expectations shape how she presents herself and interacts with others?

2. **The mystery surrounding Alaric La Croix's disappearance remains unresolved throughout the novel.**
   How does this uncertainty influence Madison's understanding of her family and her own identity?

3. **Lydia, Abigail, and Madison each rely on different strengths—charisma, intellect, or observation.**
   How do these differences shape their friendship, and what tensions emerge between them over

time?

4. **Privilege plays an important role in the story.**
   In what ways does privilege protect the characters, and in what ways does it limit them?

5. **Eli, the boy from Resonance, represents a world outside Madison's expectations and structures.**
   What does their connection reveal about the parts of Madison's life that feel most genuine?

6. **Several characters perform roles expected of them—heir, socialite, loyal friend, dutiful daughter.**
   Which characters seem most aware of these roles, and which seem most trapped by them?

7. **As Madison matures, she begins to see the world with greater clarity, recognizing the motives and insecurities that shape people's behavior.**
   Do you view this change as empowerment, a loss of innocence, or something more complicated?

8. **Aunt Mattie often challenges the emotional restraint that defines the La Croix family.**
   How does her perspective influence Madison's understanding of strength, control, and vulnerability?

9. **The novel suggests that people often maintain social systems even when they recognize their flaws.**
Why do you think those systems endure?

10. **The novel ends with Madison making a choice that the reader never fully sees—only that it costs her everything.**
What do you believe she chose, and what moments in the story led you to that conclusion?

www.ingramcontent.com/pod-product-compliance
Lightning Source LLC
Chambersburg PA
CBHW051427130726
47987CB00005B/1954